EASY LOVIN'

I've been with a lot of women, Liz..." he said.

She began to undress and said, "That sounds like a confession."

"It is."

Fully nude she approached him and put her hands on his shoulders.

"All we owe each other right now is some pleasure and some relaxation. All right?"

For his answer he reached for her breasts, and she closed her eyes, surprised at how gentle his touch was. She could feel his swollen tip prodding her and reached down to take it in both hands.

When he kissed her she pushed her tongue into his mouth and he slid his hands around her, down her back until they were clutching her buttocks, holding her tightly to him. She slid one hand up his side and could feel the outline of his ribs.

"You could use some extra weight," she said, teasing him.

"It would slow me down . . ."

She lifted her arms and said, "Come on, Alex. I want you."

That was the best news he'd heard in a long time.

ANGEL EYES

#5

LOGAN'S ARMY

Also by Robert J. Randisi

Angel Eyes
- #1: The Miracle of Revenge
- #2: Death's Angel
- #3: Wolf Pass
- #4: Chinatown Justice
- #5: Logan's Army
- #6: Bullets and Bad Times
- #7: Six Gun Angel
- #8: Avenging Angel
- #9: Angel for Hire

Tracker
- #1: The Winning Hand
- #2: Lincoln County
- #3: The Blue Cut Job
- #4: Chinatown Chance
- #5: Oklahoma Score

Mountain Jack Pike
- #1: Mountain Jack Pike
- #2: Rocky Mountain Kill
- #3: Comanche Come-On
- #4: Crow Bait
- #5: Green River Hunt

ANGEL EYES

#5

LOGAN'S ARMY

Robert J. Randisi

SPEAKING VOLUMES, LLC

NAPLES, FLORIDA

2012

ANGEL EYES

#5 LOGAN'S ARMY

ISBN 978-1-61232-587-3

For Christopher and Matthew
You can read this when you're eighteen

CHAPTER ONE

Liz Archer directed Blossom, her bay mare, down the main street of Loganville, Wyoming, at midday and saw a thriving, growing town. For each ongoing, successful business appearing on the street, there was a new place opening in a freshly constructed building. One such business appeared to be a saloon whose clapboard front was spotless and almost shining. The ornate sign hanging above the entrance announced in startling colors of pink and purple that it was *Honey's Place*.

Heads turned as she continued on down the street, but she was used to that. She only hoped they were looking at her because of her beauty and not because they recognized her. The orange bandana that had become the trademark of "Angel Eyes" was tucked away inside her collar, so the chances were good that it was the golden hair falling to her shoulders from beneath her hat, and the lovely, full figure that was drawing the attention of interested men and envious women.

Liz rode on until she found the livery, where she turned Blossom over to the care of the liveryman. During her sojourn down the town's main street she had seen several hotels and had already decided at which she would stay. During the walk back she once again passed Honey's Place, but a stop at the saloon would come later. Right now her priorities were a room and a bath.

Among the eyes watching Liz Archer ride down the main street of Loganville were Mike Early's. Early worked for Ed Logan, but he did not pal around with the rest of Logan's men. He wasn't like the rest of them. For one thing, he was better educated. As a matter of fact, at one time he was a school teacher back East. For another thing, he considered his morals higher than theirs, and he did not accompany them on their frequent visits to Sadie's, because he did not pay for sex.

For a healthy, strapping young man of thirty-five, Mike Early thought very little about sex in general. That is, until he first laid eyes on Liz Archer.

She chose neither the largest nor the smallest hotel, hoping that the rates would be reasonable, and a bath readily available. When her inquiries were answered to satisfaction, she registered and took her saddlebags to her room. Unpacking some fresh clothing she went back downstairs to use the bath facilities.

Following the desk clerk's instructions she went through a curtained doorway and down a hall, where she found the bathroom. As she entered, she realized immediately that she was not alone in the room.

"Oh," the woman in one of the tubs said, turning her head to see who had entered. "You gave me a scare."

"I'm sorry," Liz said. "The clerk didn't tell me there was someone back here."

"That's okay," the woman said. "There's hot water there, but you've got to fill your own tub."

"As long as it's hot," Liz said, putting her fresh clothing down on a chair.

"You can go ahead and undress, honey," the woman said. "It's just us girls here."

Liz smiled briefly and unbuttoned her shirt. She undressed to her undies and then filled her tub three-quarters of the way. That done, she stripped naked under the frank appraisal of the other woman and stepped in.

"If you don't mind me saying so," the woman said as Liz began to soap herself, "you've got a beautiful body."

"Thank you," Liz said, wondering if she was going to have to repel an advance from the woman.

"You wouldn't be looking for a job while you're in town, would you?"

"Not really."

"Pity," she said. "We could use a woman like you."

"Where?"

"I work at Sadie's House," the woman answered, "and you can guess what kind of house that is."

"I suppose I can."

"Not looking down your nose at me, are you?"

"No," Liz said, "I'm not in any position to do that."

"I didn't think so," the other woman said. "You don't seem the stuck-up type. I'm Angela Pettibone, if you can believe that."

"Liz Archer."

Their tubs were close enough together for the women to exchange a soggy handshake.

"I go by Angela Petty when I'm working."

"I go by Liz Archer."

"What do you do, Liz?"

"I travel," Liz said and to herself added, and right now I'd like to take a bath in peace.

As if reading her mind Angela said, "Well, I've got to get to work, so . . ."

She stood up and stepped out of the tub, and Liz got a good look at her. She had long dark hair, dark eyebrows, and a wide, sensuous mouth. Her breasts were beautifully large and firm with dark brown nipples. They were her best feature, for her waist was a little too thick and her thighs somewhat fleshy — although Liz doubted that a man would be as critical. Angela Pettibone appeared to be in her mid-thirties, the picture of an aging prostitute, but one who was aging fairly well.

Liz avoided watching the woman while she dressed and then, from the door, Angela said, "Well, if you change your mind come on over to Sadie's and tell her I sent you."

"I'll remember."

"See you around."

"Sure."

After the woman left Liz applied her full attention to a long, leisurely bath.

In the street Angela ran into Ed Logan, the man who practically owned Loganville, and for whom it was named.

"Angela, honey," he said, gripping her by the shoulders with powerful hands.

Logan was a tall, barrel-chested man in his forties, good looking and forceful, and extremely wealthy. Angela was grateful for the fact that, for the past year, she had been his favorite girl from Sadie's, and that he often sent for her to come to his suite for private parties.

She still treated him with the utmost respect, however, despite the fact that they had been as intimate — physically — as a man and woman can be.

"Hello, Mr. Logan."

"Now I've told you about that Mr. Logan stuff, Angela," Logan said. "Call me Ed."

"All right . . . Ed."

"Are you in a hurry?"

"I've got to get to work."

Logan leaned close to her and took a deep breath.

"Fresh from a bath, I see."

"Yes."

A couple of women from the town passed by and tossed disapproving glances at the two of them. Angela saw them and smiled inside. Logan simply ignored them.

"Well, I don't want to keep you from your work," he said, releasing the strong hold he had on her. "I'll see you . . . soon."

"I hope so, Mr. Logan."

As she moved past him he looked after her, wishing that she hadn't begun to show her age. She still had beautiful breasts of course, but soon they'd begin to go as well. For the present, however, she was still the one he preferred. There was only one other woman in town who tickled his fancy as much — or more — than Angela did, but she was still playing hard to get.

Soon, though, very soon, he expected that to change.

CHAPTER TWO

Bathed, dressed in fresh clothes, and feeling vaguely human again after a week on the trail, Liz's next stop was Honey's Place. She wanted a quick drink before finding someplace to eat. She rarely spent much time in a saloon, because invariably some man — drunk or sober — took it into his head to approach her. She was usually able to handle these irritations without problems, but there were those odd times when an irritation turned into unavoidable trouble. She could have stopped going into saloons altogether, but that would have been giving up, and giving up was against her nature.

She picked Honey's Place because it had caught her eye as she came into town. She stepped inside and saw that it was a large place with plenty of tables for the customers to sit and drink at, and plenty of gaming tables as well, all of which were being staffed by women. There was also a woman bartender behind the bar and, of course, saloon girls circulating among the customers. In the center of the ceiling was a large, crystal chandelier.

Whoever owned the place obviously had the right idea in using women in all the positions, because the place was packed with men, and the women certainly had to be part of the appeal. She wondered if the women went any farther than their assigned jobs, or if that was left strictly up to the girls at Sadie's.

She walked to the bar, more secure than she might have been in other saloons. There were plenty of women around to occupy the attention of the men, and maybe she wouldn't have a problem during her drink.

She ordered a beer and began to consume it leisurely. It was about half gone when the old problem suddenly reared its ugly head. She felt a heavy hand on her shoulder and turned in time for a breath of fetid air to strike her in the face.

"Hiya, honey," the man said. He was bleary eyed and unshaven, and smelled like he hadn't had a bath in years. "You all alone here?"

"Yes," she said, moving her shoulder out from under his hand, "and I want to stay that way."

"Oooh," the man said, "stuck-up, huh?"

"Look, mister . . ." she said wearily, but suddenly a woman with one of the saloon girls in tow appeared on the other side of the man.

"Here, Casey," she said, pulling the man around by his elbow, "talk to Lisa and leave the customers alone, all right?"

"Sure, Honey," the man said, "this one's too good for the likes of me, anyway."

The saloon girl, Lisa, linked her arm in the cowboy's and lead him away.

"You pay for that beer yet?" the woman asked Liz.

"As soon as I get the bartender's attention."

"Forget it, it's on the house."

"You authorized to give drinks away?"

"I should be," the woman said, smiling, "I own the place." Sticking her hand out she added, "I'm Honey O'Day. Welcome to Honey's Place."

Liz shook the woman's hand and studied her briefly. She was in her mid-thirties, big breasted and pretty, with honey colored hair and a small mole at one corner of her mouth. She was about the same age as Angela Pettibone, but carrying it a little better. Maybe that's because Angela was still a working girl, and Honey had been smart enough to go into management.

"You've got a nice place here."

"Thanks."

"You seem to be offering something other places don't."

"If you mean my girls," she said, "their only jobs are what you see them doing now. Anything else is up to them. Still, having a lot of pretty girls around does bring the customers in."

"No trouble?"

"Not so far, but we've only been open . . . let's see, how long is it? About a month. As for trouble, there hasn't been anything I haven't been able to handle up to now."

"Do you have female bouncers, too?"

Honey laughed and said, "Oh, if it comes to that we can always rustle up a man or two, don't you think?"

Looking around, Liz said, "I'm sure you could."

"You just ride in?"

"Yes."

"Passing through?"

"Yes."

"A job offer wouldn't interest you, would it?"

"I'm having a busy day," Liz said.

"What do you mean?"

"This is the second job offer I've had."

"Who was the other one from?"

"A girl named Angela asked if I'd like to work at a place called Sadie's House."

"Oh, . . . Sadie's," Honey said. "Those girls offer a little more complete services than mine do."

"Are you competitors?"

"In a way, but Sadie doesn't have the gambling we do, and men like to gamble almost as much as they like to . . . if you get my meaning."

"I do."

"Well, what did you say to that job?"

"Same thing I'm saying to yours, thanks but no thanks."

"Then if I can't offer you a job, how about another beer?"

"That offer I'll take you up on."

Honey waved to the bartender and said, "Another beer here, Lori."

The bartender brought it over and Liz noticed that

she looked remarkably like the other girl, Lisa. They both had dark hair, slender figures and appeared to be nineteen or twenty years old.

"She should, they're twins. I wanted Lori as my bartender, but I had to take Lisa, as well. Lori's a marvelous bartender, but Lisa's talents lie in . . . other areas. Sadie's been trying to hire Lisa away, but you can't have one without the other."

"Seems to have worked out in your favor."

"I usually try to make sure they do. Enjoy your stay . . ."

"Liz, Liz Archer."

"Enjoy your stay, Liz, and I'm afraid if you want another beer after that one you'll have to pay for it."

Liz raised the mug she had in her hand in a sort of salute and said, "That sounds fair."

"And if you change your mind about the job . . ."

"You'll be the first to know."

There was an awkward moment then, when Honey simply stood there staring at Liz as if she were trying to place her, but then the woman smiled, patted Liz's arm and turned her attention to her other customers.

Liz finished the beer, then called Lori over and asked her where there was a good place to eat.

"Go down the street a couple of blocks until you reach Sackett Street. There's a cafe there that's real good."

"Thanks."

"Sure, come back again later."

"I'll do that."

And she would, too. Honey's Place was about the

friendliest saloon she'd ever been in, and she was sure that the place, and the woman, would be a success in Loganville.

CHAPTER THREE

Liz ate in the cafe and, as Lori had promised, found the food "real good." When she left the place she decided to go right back to the saloon, rather than check out some of the other establishments in town. She doubted that she would find a place to match Honey's.

As she pushed through the batwing doors she immediately became aware of the tension in the place. She stepped hastily to one side so she could observe and find out what was going on.

A tableau occurring in the center of the room held everyones attention. It consisted of two men, one with a knife drawn. He was holding the knife against the faro dealer's pretty throat and standing opposite him was Honey. As Liz listened, she realized that the saloon owner was trying to reason with him.

"Look, mister," she was saying, "I'll give you

back all the money you lost, just don't hurt Sheila. She's the best dealer I've got."

"Ha!" the man shouted. "If you're gonna give us back our money that means she was cheatin'."

"We don't cheat here, mister," Honey assured him, "but if that's what you want to think, go ahead. Just let her go."

The girl was staring at Honey through frightened eyes, and Liz could tell from Honey's tone that the older woman was trying to soothe her fears as much as she was trying to reason with the two irate men.

Sheila, the dealer, was a dark-haired woman in her mid-twenties, slight of build and dwarfed by the man who was holding her with one arm around her breasts and a sharp knife to her throat. Slowly, so as not to attract attention, Liz began to ease between the men standing in front of her, so she'd be in front of them instead of behind them. She wondered if anyone had gone for the law.

"Oh no," the man went on, "I want to hear you say it. Tell all of these people that you was cheatin' me."

"They'll know it's not true."

"Say it, or I'll cut her throat!"

From the way the man was standing he couldn't see Lori, the bartender, who was easing over the top of the bar, a wicked looking length of wood in her hand. Liz wondered if the girl had a shotgun back there, but had decided against using it.

"Look, mister . . ." Honey said.

"Say it, bitch!"

The man's partner was standing with his hand on his gun, grinning at the goings on. He turned slightly to his right, just enough so that he spotted Lori and her piece of wood, easing towards him.

"Jackson!" he shouted, and at that point Lori made her move. She sprinted towards the shouting man, who started to go for his gun, but she let him have it over the head with the length of wood and he slumped to the ground.

His partner, seeing what had happened, decided to ignore Honey, release Sheila, and go after Lori.

"Bitch!" he shouted, using what appeared to be a favorite word of his. He pushed Sheila towards Honey, who caught her, and raised his knife as if to throw it at Lori, who was wide open.

Liz took two steps forward, drew her gun and fired. The knife flew from the man's hand and he cried out, bringing his stinging fingers to his mouth. He took them away long enough to look for blood and when he found none put them back to his mouth anyway.

At that point the batwing doors opened and two men stepped in. Both were wearing badges, one a sheriff's badge and the other a deputy's.

"What's going on here?" the sheriff demanded. He was a tall, thin man with a big, bushy gray mustache, and he had his hand resting on the worn Colt in his holster.

"About time you got here, Sheriff," Honey O'Day said. She had her arms around Sheila protectively, and the girl seemed to have a bad case of the shakes.

The sheriff came forward and Honey quickly explained what had happened.

"Who fired the shot?" he demanded, looking around.

Liz, her gun back in her holster, had used the sheriff's arrival to fade back behind a group of men, and the sheriff stared at the roomful of people expectantly and frowned when he didn't get an answer.

"I want to know who fired that shot!"

"What does it matter who fired, Sheriff Keane?" Honey asked, handing Sheila over to the care of the sisters, Lisa and Lori. "I want these two men arrested."

"Now, ma'am, I'm sure they didn't mean any harm. They was probably just all likkered up — "

"And they work for Ed Logan," Honey finished for him in disgust. "I know the story, Sheriff. I'd appreciate it if you'd get them out of here."

"I can do that," the man said. The man on the floor was still out cold so the sheriff got some help and removed both men from the premises.

It took only seconds for the customers to drift back to what they had been doing before the excitement, and Liz noticed that Honey replaced Sheila at the faro table and allowed Lisa to walk the girl upstairs, probably taking her to her room to relax. The other twin, Lori, had already returned to her place behind the bar.

Liz walked to the bar and waited her turn before ordering a beer.

Lori, recognizing her, said, "Got back just in time for the excitement, huh?"

"You swing a mean piece of wood, but don't you have a shotgun back there?"

"Sure, but if I cut loose with it I might have hit somebody else, too."

"Good point."

"Sure wish I knew who fired that shot."

Ignoring the remark Liz started to dig into her pocket for the money for the beer but from behind her Honey O'Day said, "Lori, this lady's drinks are on the house from now on."

"Yes, ma'am," Lori said, and moved to the other end of the bar to serve a customer.

"That's very kind — " Liz started to say, but the older woman cut her off.

"I'd like to talk to you in my office, if I can," Honey said, interrupting her.

"Is this about that job?"

"It's about *a* job," Honey replied, "but not the same one."

"I'm really not interested in any job at the moment, Miss O'Day."

"You fired that shot, Liz," Honey said.

After a moment Liz said, "So?"

"How'd you like the sheriff to know that the famous Angel Eyes is in his town?" Honey asked in a low voice.

"What do you want?"

"I want you to bring your beer and come into my office," Honey said, and then turned and walked away, not bothering to check to see if Liz was following.

Which she was.

CHAPTER FOUR

"Please close the door behind you," Honey O'Day said as Liz entered. "Have a seat."

Seeing that Liz had left her beer at the bar Honey asked, "Can I offer you something? I have some good brandy."

"Brandy'd be fine," Liz said, "and then I'd like an explanation."

"I fully intend to give you one," Honey said, pouring out two brandies and handing Liz one. She took the other and seated herself behind her desk with it.

"I need help."

"What kind of help?" Liz asked.

"Your kind, the kind you gave us out there — and don't think I'm not grateful for it."

"You have a funny way of showing it."

"I know. I'm sorry, but when I realized who you were . . . I just saw it as the answer I've been looking for."

"The answer to what?"

"My problem."

"Which is?"

"Edward Logan."

Liz started to ask "Who?", then stopped and said instead, "Of *Logan*ville?"

"The same."

"What's your problem with him?"

"When I came here I didn't know that he ran the town."

"How much of the town?"

"Most of the people, and any of the businesses that make money."

"Except yours."

"Right."

"And he wants it?"

"Right again."

"So he does things like sending those two in here to disrupt things."

Honey O'Day nodded.

"What do you need me for?"

"To do what you did tonight."

"You mean use my gun to protect you from him?"

"Right."

"I'm sorry, Miss O'Day—"

"Call me Honey."

"Miss O'Day," Liz said again, "I don't hire out my gun."

"But I thought . . . I mean, your reputation . . ."

"A reputation is the smallest part of a person," Liz said. "I mean, of the real person."

"I can pay you . . ."

"I'm sorry," Liz said again, standing up.

"Couldn't you think about it?" Honey asked. "Overnight?"

"I could," Liz said, "but I doubt that I'd change my mind."

"All I ask is that you consider it."

Liz hesitated, then because she liked the woman said, "All right, Miss O'Day. I'll consider it."

"And you'll call me Honey?"

"Sure . . . Honey."

The two men who had caused the commotion in Honey's Place were at that moment standing before Ed Logan's desk. That is, one was standing and the other, still suffering from the effects of the blow on the head, was slumping. His name was Jackson, while the other man, the one who had brandished the knife, was Scott.

"Tell me that again, Scott," Logan said in a low, controlled tone of voice. "The knife was shot out of your hand by a woman?"

"Yeah," Scott said, "I saw her just before the sheriff came in."

"And you were hit on the head by a woman?" Logan asked Jackson, who was only able to nod — an action that caused him considerable pain.

"Get out of here Jackson, before you keel over," Logan said, disgusted.

Scott also began to move towards the door, but Logan stopped him cold.

"Not you, Scott."

Scott retraced the few steps he'd taken and stood in front of his employer's desk again.

"I want you to do two things for me, Scott."

"What?"

"I want you to find out about the woman with the gun."

"And?"

"And," Logan said, leaning forward, "I want you to pay back the girl who hit Jackson. She's the one who really messed things up, and I want her to feel a little of what Jackson's feeling."

"How far can we go, sir?" Scott asked, remembering what the bartender looked like.

"Don't kill her," Logan said. "Beyond that, it's up to you."

"Yes, sir!"

They were waiting for her after Honey's Place closed. She left by the front door and started down the street, but they quickly grabbed her and hustled her down a deep alley, away from the lamp posts, where it was black as coal.

The three of them pinned her to the ground, one holding her legs, another her arms, and the third — Scott — putting a hand over her mouth. Pretty soon they all had night vision and were able to see each other.

"Pretty," one man said.

"More than that," Scott replied, looking down at the young woman with obvious lust. "Get her clothes off."

There was some tearing of fabric and her clothing came away, underwear and all, until she was naked. Her breasts seemed to glow, so pale was her skin, and her nipples were small and dark.

"Nice," Scott said, putting one hand over her right breast, "real nice. Hold her steady, I'm gonna fuck her."

"And then us?" the third man asked, hopefully.

"We won't have time," Scott said, positioning between her widespread legs.

"You bastard," she managed to mutter behind a dirty hand.

Scott reached between his legs to finger his cock and, when it was standing straight and hard, he rammed it into her. He was disappointed that she didn't make a sound, and he began to pound into her, wanting her to cry or moan or something, but she never did. She lay there and took it, staring at him defiantly while he emptied himself into her.

"You bitch," he said afterward, tucking himself back into his pants. "That's the best you ever had, ain't it? Take your hand away from her mouth," he told one of the other men, "I wanna hear her say it."

The hand came away from her mouth and she said, "You've got to be kidding. I've had handshakes from kids that were better than that."

"You rotten, lying bitch!" Scott said, slapping her hard across the face.

That was just the first blow, and by the time he was done, there was no need for the other two men to hold her down anymore.

Nobody had to hold down Angela Pettibone for Ed Logan. She was on her back on his bed, naked, and he was running his lips and tongue lovingly over her breasts and nipples when there was a knock on his door.

"Damn," he said. He smiled at Angela and said, "I'll be right back."

"No hurry," she said, and when he looked at her funny she added, "I'm not going anywhere."

She watched him walk from the bedroom into the other room of his suite, putting on his robe, and then she sat up. She had to watch what she said to him; she didn't want him thinking that she didn't love being with him.

Actually, the truth of the matter was she didn't love being with any man. Since an early age men hadn't interested Angela as anything other than a means to her own end. Of course that had never worked out very well; otherwise she wouldn't have ended up a whore. As for Ed Logan, she saw him as her last chance to get out of the business, and she didn't want to mess it up. It had to be now, with him, because she wasn't getting any younger.

She laid back down on the bed and decided that when he came back and started slobbering over her again, she was going to close her eyes and think of Liz Archer's smooth skin and pink-tipped breasts.

Logan opened his door angrily and saw Scott standing there.

"What is it?"

Scott started at the tone in his boss's voice and said, "If I'm interrupting . . ."

"Just tell me what you want."

"I just wanted to tell you that me and the boys took care of that gal from the saloon. You know, that bartender . . ."

"Fine, now get lost for a few days."

"Sure, boss."

As Scott started away Logan grabbed his arm and said, "You didn't kill her, did you?"

"No boss, you said not to."

"All right. Take whoever you got to help you and get lost," he said, again.

"Right."

Logan closed his door, dropped his robe to the floor in front of it and stared down at his erection. It hadn't lost any of its size or hardness during the interruption, and he went back into the bedroom to give Angela Pettibone the full benefit of its power.

CHAPTER FIVE

As she had promised Honey O'Day, Liz had considered her offer overnight. As much as she liked the woman, and her place, she just didn't want to hire her gun out. It was a bad habit to get into. Also, she'd had enough of buying into other people's problems.

She went downstairs and decided that before checking out she would stop at that little cafe again, this time for breakfast. She would also stop by Honey's Place and give Honey O'Day her final decision.

After breakfast she knocked on the front door of Honey's Place and kept knocking until it was finally answered by a woman she didn't recognize.

"I'd like to see Honey."

"She ain't seeing anybody this morning," the woman answered. She was a tall, willowy redhead with pale skin and freckles, and even without makeup she was lovely. Honey certainly knew what kind of girls to hire.

"It'll only take a minute."

"Can't."

Liz, sensing something was wrong, asked the woman. "What's wrong?"

"One of our girls got hurt last night," the redhead said, "bad. She's upstairs."

"What do you mean, hurt?"

"I mean beaten up and raped. We found her in the alley last night, naked."

"Look, I've got to see Honey," Liz said, pushing past the redhead.

"Fine," the woman said, offering little resistance. "Let her tell you to get lost."

Liz crossed the floor, skirting the tables with the chairs piled atop them, and hurried up the steps.

"Honey!" she called out, looking up and down the hall. "Honey O'Day!"

A door opened and Honey stepped out, looking haggard, tired, and older.

"What do you want?"

"I heard one of your girls got hurt."

"That's right."

"Who?"

Honey beckoned her over and swung open the door to the room she'd come out of. Liz entered. In the bed was a dark haired girl, her face bruised and cut. Next to her, holding her hand, was her twin.

"Lori?" Liz asked.

The other girl looked up, her face streaked with tears, and said, "Lisa. It was supposed to be me I suppose, because of what I did last night, but whoever did this couldn't tell us apart."

"They hurt the wrong girl," Honey said.

Liz turned to her and said, "Have you spoken to the sheriff?"

"Sure I did. He said he'll do whatever he can, which means nothing. He's in Ed Logan's pocket, and Logan's men did this."

Liz looked at the young woman again and winced at the swollen, purple marks on her face, some of which had split and bled.

"Come outside," Honey said.

"Has she been seen by a doctor?"

"Yes," Honey said, then touched Liz's arm and said, "Outside."

In the hall Honey said, "Walk to my room with me." As they walked she said, "Actually they didn't get the wrong girl at all."

"What do you mean?"

"If this *had* happened to Lori instead of her sister, she would have died. She wouldn't have survived it, especially the rape. Lisa's tougher than Lori, and the rape doesn't really bother her, not when she's done that for a living."

"And Lori?"

"Lori's a virgin, Liz," Honey said, "if you can believe that. The rape would have caused her to lose her mind. Even Lisa said it once during the night. She's glad it happened to her and not to her sister."

At the door to her room Honey said, "I've got to take a bath and try to make myself look human."

"What are you going to do about this?" Liz asked.

"What can I do? They'll get away with it. Logan's men get away with anything."

"But they may kill one of your girls next time."

"The girls all know that. They're free to go if they want to."

"And?"

"None of them are," Honey said with a satisfied look on her face. "God knows, I love them all."

Honey opened her door and started to go in when Liz stopped her.

"Honey?"

"Yes?"

"I've decided to take you up on your offer."

"I'm glad, Liz," Honey said, "but could we talk price later, in my office?"

"No, let's talk about it now."

Honey stared at Liz, frowning.

"You mean . . ."

"I mean no price," Liz said. "I'll work for you for nothing just to see that Logan and his men get what's coming to them."

"You've got to accept something."

"That would mean I was hiring out my gun, Honey," Liz said. "I told you, I don't do that."

Honey took Liz's hand and said, "I appreciate this, Liz, and my girls will, too."

"I'm sorry one of them had to get hurt . . ."

"Don't be taking the blame for that," Honey said, squeezing Liz's hand and then letting go. "Let's just take it from here and see what we can accomplish. All right?"

"All right."

"Now go and get your stuff. I have an empty room

that you can have." Liz started to argue but Honey said, "The least I can give you is room and board. You can accept that, can't you?"

"Sure. I'll see you in a bit."

Liz started down the hall to the stairs and stopped when the door to Lisa's room opened and Lori stepped out.

"How is she?"

"She's asleep."

Lori looked like she could use some of that herself, and Liz told her so.

"I'll just take a bath and be fine," she insisted. "I don't want to leave her alone for too long. Honey told me who you really are, Liz, and that she offered you a job here helping us."

"And she told you I turned her down?"

"Yes."

"Well, now she'll tell you that I decided to stay and help, for room and board."

"That's all?"

"I don't like what happened to your sister, Lori, and when Logan and his men realize that it *was* your sister and not you. . . . I want to make sure it doesn't happen to you, too — or to any of the other girls."

"And you'll try and find out who raped my sister?"

Liz was no detective, but the look on the girl's face was so plaintive she simply said, "Yes."

Lori surprised Liz then. She threw her arms around her, gave her a big hug, and kissed her on the cheek.

"Thank you, Liz."

Embarrassed, Liz said, "I have to get my stuff from the hotel. I'll see you a little later."

"All right."

Lori went into her room, which was right next to her sister's, and Liz went back downstairs and outside. She'd gone and done it again, dealt herself into somebody else's hand — and a bad hand, at that.

When Liz Archer came out of Honey's Place and started for the hotel Ed Logan was standing at the window of his office across the street with his man, Jackson, at his side.

"That's her, Boss!" Jackson said, pointing anxiously, "that's the gal."

"Mother of God," Logan said, staring at her in awe. He watched her intently until she was out of sight.

CHAPTER SIX

By the time Liz reclaimed her gear, checked out of the hotel, and returned to Honey's Place, Honey O'Day had bathed and fixed her face so that the worry lines were well hidden behind a layer of makeup. Liz revised her original opinion of Honey's age, putting it closer to forty.

"I'll show you your room," Honey said. She led Liz down the hall and gave her the room all the way at the end.

"It's the only empty I've got."

"It's fine," Liz said, and it was more than fine. It was better than she'd found in most hotels throughout the West, and to find a more comfortable bed she'd probably have to go all the way back to San Francisco.

"There are bathtubs down at the other end of the

hall, and we have a boy who fills the tubs. I'd appreciate it if you'd give him a little something afterward.''

"Sure," Liz replied, hoping that Honey was talking about money.

"When you're settled in come downstairs and I'll
introduce you to the others.''

Liz didn't have to do much to settle in, but she
decided to take a bath so it was about an hour before
she finally got downstairs. The boy Honey had alluded
to turned out to be a gangly kid of about fifteen, and
he seemed disappointed when Liz gave him ten cents
for filling her bathtub.

"Ah, here's Liz now," Honey said as Liz came
down.

Apparently Honey had gathered all of her em-
ployees together to introduce them to Liz and explain
her presence.

"Some of you already know Liz. For those of you
who don't, she's going to be our bodyguard against
Ed Logan and his men.''

"You're kidding.''

The speaker was the redhead that had answered
Liz's knock that morning.

"No, Trina, I'm not," Honey said, giving the
woman a sharp glance.

Liz already knew Lisa and Lori, who were upstairs
in Lisa's room, and she remembered Sheila, the faro
dealer, from the night before. There were three other
house dealer's, an auburn haired woman named Belle
and a woman who had prematurely silver hair, named

Ellen. Belle was in her twenties, tall and slender, like Trina, but not quite as classy looking. Ellen appeared to be the oldest of the women who worked for Honey, but she still wasn't old enough to have earned her silver hair. She kept it beautifully, however, and was quite a handsome woman.

Trina's name was Katrina, and she seemed to feel as if she were the belle of the ball, so to speak. She even stood off to one side so that she was separate from the other girls.

Honey had two other girls whose job, like Lisa's, was to simply circulate among the men. The two were women in their twenties. Rita was a chunky redhead about five feet tall, and Sandy was a black girl with lovely, smooth skin and full, sensuous lips.

At this hour of the morning all of the girls were simply attired in a robe or wrapper of some kind, from Sheila's quilted robe to Trina's diaphanous wrapper.

"All right, girls," Honey said, "now that you've met Liz just remember, if there's any trouble look to her for help."

"How's Lisa?" Sheila asked.

"Lisa's going to be fine," Honey said, and then directing herself to all the girls added, "and Liz is here to make sure nothing like that ever happens again."

"Well," Rita said, "I for one feel safer with her around. I saw her make that shot last night."

Liz wondered just how many people did see her make that shot — a damned foolish shot at that —

and had kept quiet when the sheriff started asking about it. If Tate Gilmore ever saw her try a trick shot like that he'd break her arm.

"You made that shot?" Trina asked in disbelief.

"I may have been lucky."

"That's a lot of crap," Sandy, the black girl, said. "Sweetie, ah'll bet you make that shot nine out of ten times, if not moah."

"All right, girls, that's enough," Honey said. "Let's get ready for a busy day."

The girls dispersed, some of them making a point of welcoming Liz aboard. As the last of them filed up the stairs Liz moved over next to Honey.

"Thanks for not mentioning . . . who I am."

"There's no need for that," Honey said, "and we wouldn't want it to get around town. It might bring in the wrong element. Is there anything you need?"

"Have you got access to some workmen?"

"I've got money," Honey said, "that gives me access to just about anything I need."

"Good. I want you to build me something . . ."

Sheriff Johnny Keane knocked on Ed Logan's door and opened it.

"You wanted to see me, Mr. Logan."

"Yes, Johnny, come on in and shut the door," Logan said from behind his desk.

Keane did as he was told and presented himself in front of Logan's desk.

"Johnny," Logan said, "I want you and your deputies to stay away from Honey's Place for awhile."

"Hey, that trouble last night wasn't my fault, Mr. Logan . . . "

"No, no, you don't understand," Logan said. "I don't blame you for anything, Johnny. I'm just looking to protect you, to protect your job."

"I don't understand."

"Well, there might be trouble at Honey's Place for a while, and I don't want you in the middle of it."

"But what do I tell the townspeople if I'm not around when there's trouble?"

"You'll think of something, Johnny," Ed Logan said. "I have confidence in you. Just stay away from that saloon. Do you understand?"

"Yes, Mr. Logan. I understand."

"Good. That's all."

Keane turned and left Logan's office, stopping in the hall to take a deep breath. For a moment he'd thought he was going to lose his cushy job as sheriff of Loganville. Instead, Logan wanted him *not* to do that job, and he certainly could do that!

Several hours later, after the highly paid hard work of a few men with carpentry skills, Honey and Liz stared up at the structure that had been built.

"You can see everything that goes on in the room from up there," Honey said.

"That's the general idea."

They were staring at a wooden platform that was set in the wall high enough so that, if she wanted to, Liz could touch the ceiling. Built flat against the wall was a wooden ladder to allow her easy access to the platform.

"I've seen this in a lot of cow towns and boom towns where every night in a saloon was an adventure. I can sit up there with a rifle or a shotgun and nip trouble in the bud before it ever gets started."

"Well," Honey said, putting her hands on her hips, "I can see that if I *was* paying you, you'd be worth whatever amount it was."

CHAPTER SEVEN

Mike Early got the word that Ed Logan wanted to see him and wondered why. When he arrived at his employer's office however, he found that it wasn't just he who had been called. Early was the seventh man to arrive.

"Early," Logan said as he entered, "do you know where Pennell is?"

"I could probably guess."

If Early *did* have a friend among Logan's other men, it would be Pennell — which was odd, because the two men were nothing alike. The only reason that Early thought he might know where Pennell was, was because he knew that Pennell spent every spare moment he could at Sadie's. He'd never known a man so obsessed with women — all women, no matter what shape or form.

"They're all the same lying down in the dark,

Mike,'' Pennell had once told him, and he found it strange that then he had seen some truth in that. He didn't, anymore. Not since he'd seen that blonde who'd ridden into town. She *couldn't* be like anyone else, lying down, standing up, in the dark or the light.

"Well?'' Logan said.

"Well what?''

"Well, go and get him. I want you all here . . . and fast.''

"All right.''

Early didn't exchange glances with anyone else in the room before he left to find Alex Pennell.

"He's a strange one,'' Mark Tanner said. Tanner was Logan's right-hand man. If the town boss had a ranch, Tanner would be his foreman. The man was in his late thirties and he was perfect for the position he was in — one of authority, but not the top spot. He was tough enough to tell Ed Logan to take his money and shove it.

"What do you mean?'' Logan asked.

"He doesn't fit in, Mr. Logan.''

"You hired him.''

"I know I did,'' Tanner said, "but even I can make a mistake once in a while.''

"Well, I can't afford to lose him now,'' Logan said. "Not with Scott and Jackson and two others out of town.''

"What's so important?''

"I'll tell you what's so important — making sure that my position in this town isn't undermined.''

Tanner wasn't sure he knew what his boss meant, but he didn't want to let on.

"Oh."

"I'll explain it better when Early gets back with Pennell." Logan looked at Tanner intently and said, "You don't have any second thoughts about Pennell, do you?"

"His brain is below his belt," Tanner said, bringing a laugh from the other men in the room, "but he's all right."

"Good," Logan said, "I wouldn't want to hear of you making *too many* mistakes."

Mike Early found Pennell just where he thought he would, nestled between the thighs of a woman in Sadie's House.

"He's upstairs," Sadie said, as she recognized Early.

Sadie was a carefully kept fifty with big breasts and spreading hips. Her face was covered with so much powder and rouge that she looked unnatural. The other girls in the place looked Early up and down, admiring the size of his shoulders, and wondering if the rest of him was in proportion.

"Thanks."

"Hey," Sadie said.

"What?" he asked, stopping on the third step.

"How come you never come around here? A lot of my girls have been dying for a try at you."

"I'll keep it in mind," Early said, deciding to keep to himself the fact that he didn't like the idea of paying for his sex. There were too many women out there willing to give it away for free.

Sadie sighed and said, "Try room six. He decided to try Big Zelda tonight."

Big Zelda, Early thought, Jesus.

Big Zelda was just that: big. As Early opened the door to room six and walked in, he saw the back of Pennell's head buried in Big Zelda's crotch. Her chubby hands were clutching the back of his head, and her fleshy thighs and breasts were jiggling as she bounced with the pressure of his mouth and tongue.

"Oooh, Alex, that's it, right there, keep doing . . . that!"

Early saw that he had arrived for the big moment. Every inch of Zelda began to jiggle now as she made a high pitched noise and began to bounce her large butt up and down on the mattress. Pennell was holding on for dear life, continuing to lick and suck hungrily, and being noisy about it himself.

"Jesus!" Zelda said as Pennell came up for air. "How'd you like it, Alex?"

Early decided to save Pennell from answering that question.

"Pennell!"

The man turned and smiled at Early.

"Mike, hey Mike. How about some of this, huh? I always was curious about fa . . . big women."

Pennell reached out and squeezed each of Zelda's breasts, and some of the flesh slipped through his fingers like dough.

"No thanks, Alex. Logan wants to see us right way. Something big is up, I guess."

"Yeah?"

Pennell got up off the bed and Early realized he was naked. He'd never seen a man built so big below the belt in his life, and the amazing thing was that

Pennell was so skinny. Still, a lot of the girls liked him because he had such a big penis, and from the looks of him he hadn't gotten his own satisfaction yet. The bulbous head was red and purple, and the entire length of him was pulsing.

"That's disgusting!" Early said, only half kidding.

"Ah, jealousy doesn't become you, my friend. What do you say, Zelda, my love? Is this disgusting?"

He moved close to the bed again so that she could reach him, and reach him she did. She grabbed his pole with both hands and stuffed the spongy head into her mouth eagerly. From there, she proceeded to ease the rest on in, inch by inch.

Winking at Mike Early, Pennell said, "I'll be with you in a few minutes, Mike. Why don't you wait downstairs?"

Thinking of all the girls downstairs, Early said, "I'll wait outside."

"It's about time," Logan said as Pennell and Early entered.

"Sorry, boss," Pennell said, "but I was getting some treatment for . . ."

"We know what you were getting treated for, Pennell," Tanner said, cutting him off. "Man, if you ever had any brains you probably fucked them out a long time ago."

"Your envy is showing, Tanner."

"That's enough. Find a seat and shut up."

Early and Pennell did as they were told, and then

there were eight men in the room waiting for Ed Logan's words.

"I want Honey's Place."

"That's a well-known fact, Boss," Tanner said.

"Is it also well-known that she won't sell?"

No one answered.

"Well, she won't, and I want it, anyway." Logan looked at each man in turn before continuing. "I want trouble at that saloon, and I want it every night. Anybody here got any objections to that?"

No one answered, although Mike Early almost did. Pennell, sensing this, nudged the other man into silence with a hard, bony elbow.

"Tanner, you coordinate it."

"How bad do you want it?"

"Don't kill anybody — but if you have to you better make it look good."

"What about the sheriff?"

"The sheriff has his instructions," Ed Logan said, "and he'll follow them. I hope that you all will follow yours. That's all. Tanner, keep me informed."

"Right, Boss. All right, boys, let's go and talk it over."

"Stay behind, Tanner. Meet them later."

The boys were anxious to go and talk it over, because the usual "talking it over" place was Sadie's parlor, after which they could go upstairs and sample the wares of Sadie's girls.

When they were out of Logan's office Early heard Pennell saying, "Let me tell you fellas about Big Zelda. I tell you, there's a woman as man hungry as she is big, and she ain't half bad . . ."

CHAPTER EIGHT

"How do I look?"

Liz was sitting up on the platform, and Honey, Sheila, and Lori were looking up at her from the floor. On the steps she could see Trina watching her, but did not acknowledge the woman's presence.

"High," Sheila said.

"Is there any part of the place you can't see from up there?" Honey asked.

"No."

"This may settle the problem inside, but what about outside, where they got my sister?" Lori asked.

"We'll have to work on that, Lori," Liz said.

"Well, you work on it," Lori said, "I'm going to check on my sister."

As Lori made for the stairs Liz used the ladder to descend back to floor level.

"She has a point, Honey," she said, "but there's only so much I can do."

"I know."

"For instance," Liz went on, "I can't stay up there from the minute you open until you close. I'd get so sleepy I'd probably fall off."

"What do you suggest?"

"Well, you tell me when your busiest hours are and on what nights, and that's when I'll sit up there. We'll just have to hope that there's no trouble during your off hours."

"I'll make you a chart," Honey said.

"Fine."

"What else?"

"Is there anyone else you could trust and hire?"

"I wouldn't know," Honey said. "This is Ed Logan's town."

"What about the boy who fills the tubs upstairs?"

"Willie? He's only fifteen . . ."

"Has he ever been with any of your girls?"

"Well, Rita's sort of sweet on him. She treats him like a pet, you know, and gives him . . . treats."

"Well, if he's man enough to handle Rita," Liz said, remembering that Rita was the short, chunky gal, "then he can help. I'll figure out how to use him."

"There might be someone else . . ." Honey said, speculatively.

"Who?"

"Well, Ed Logan's got a rotten apple in his basket."

"I'd think they were all rotten."

"I mean in reverse," Honey said, tapping her chin with the flaming red nail of her right forefinger. "There's a man who stands out in the group."

"In what way?"

"He doesn't belong there."

"You thinking maybe you could win him over to your side?"

"Well, he's a regular customer . . ."

"That doesn't answer my question," Liz said. "Who is he?"

"His name's Mike Early."

"What's he like?"

"Well, he doesn't hang around Sadie's like the others, and he doesn't bother my girls the way the others do. I get the feeling he's a more or less decent guy trying to make a living."

"Maybe you should talk to him."

"Maybe you should."

"Why?"

"In this case, I think we might be able to catch more flies with Liz Archer than we can with Honey . . ."

Across the street Mark Tanner was waiting for his boss to say what he didn't want to say in front of the others.

"Tanner, I want her liquor deliveries stopped," Logan finally said, ticking off points on his fingers, "I want her girls harassed, I want her place busted up, but I want it to look like any other bar fight."

"You really want us to lean on her, huh? Make her *want* to sell, make her *want* to come to you?"

"That's what I want."

"I guess that means you want as little damage as possible to her place?"

"Break furniture or windows, I don't care. I just want her up here asking me to become her partner . . . in more ways than one."

Tanner couldn't blame his boss for that. Honey O'Day was a lot of woman. Tanner himself took his pleasure with one of Honey's girls, although up to now they had kept their "friendship" quiet.

"One more thing, Mark," Logan said, "and then I'll let you go and talk to the men."

"What's that, Boss?"

"I want you to use only the men you trust for the more . . . delicate work. If you weren't out of town, Scott wouldn't have messed up things with that girl bartender, letting her see who he was . . ."

"You sent me out of town." Tanner's reminder to Logan was gentle and quiet. He wasn't quite sure how the other man would react to the reminder, but he did want to make certain his boss knew he wasn't going to take the blame for something that happened while he wasn't around.

"I know that, Mark," Logan assured him in a soothing tone of his own, "but now that you *are* here I want this done right."

"That's the way I always do things, Mr. Logan. I'll take care of it for you."

Logan gave his man a meaningful glance and said simply, "I hope so."

CHAPTER NINE

Over the course of the next few days nothing much happened to Honey's Place, except that her supplies had apparently been intercepted by robbers. At least, that was Sheriff Keane's guess, and he said he'd look into it. Actually nothing was stolen, it was just destroyed so that she couldn't use it.

"Did you get to talk to the man who was making the delivery?" Liz asked Honey in her office on the third day.

"I did," Honey answered. "He said he was stopped by two men wearing masks who made him get down from his wagon at gunpoint and then proceeded to shoot up my delivery. After that they left him there standing in a huge puddle of whiskey."

"What can you do?"

"What *can* I do?" Honey said helplessly. "I've got to reorder, which means I'm using twice as much money — and that's providing the second order gets through."

"Do you have enough supplies?"

"Most of the stuff, yes, but if my shipment gets hit again — by *Logan's* men, damn him — he may have just what he wants."

"You mean he wants to force you out of business?"

"He doesn't want me out of business, Liz," Honey explained, "He wants me to need *him* to stay in business."

"Honey, let me ask you something."

"What?"

"How does he know when you order supplies and when they're coming?"

"I don't know," Honey said, frowning at the papers on her desk. "He just does."

"It can't be that he *just* does. He's got someone inside."

Honey looked up and said in a resigned tone, "One of my girls."

"Who else?"

"But which one?" Honey said, as if it pained her to even ask the question.

"Would you mind an opinion?"

"Go ahead."

"Well, I haven't known any of the girls for long, but my guess would be Trina."

Honey smiled slightly and said, "There's something you should know about Trina, Liz."

"What's that?"

"Aside from Belle, she's been with me the longest."

"You trust her?"

"I've never had any reason not to. I've never had any reason to distrust *any* of my girls."

"Well," Liz said, "I'm afraid that you do now."

"Yes, I suppose I do . . ."

As Liz took her place on the platform that evening she felt as if this would be the night something would happen. She sat in her chair with her rifle across her knees and watched the action carefully. Whenever the batwing doors opened her eyes quickly went to the new customer or customers and sized them up.

Over the course of the past two evenings up on her platform she'd drawn many strange looks, but on this third night the customers seemed to have accepted her as part of the furnishings. The place was packed, and Honey pointed out, "You're an attraction now Liz, and you're pulling in even more customers for yourself to keep an eye on."

While her eyes took in everything, her mind worked on. She hadn't found a way to use Willie yet, but she would. Also, she'd had no chance to talk to or even meet Mike Early, and for a regular customer at Honey's, he was long overdue. Neither had she had a chance to meet Logan, although she'd had the man pointed out to her on the street. He had the same look as other powerful men she'd known, full of themselves and confident that nothing and no one could ever bring them down.

This man had the look and, she hoped, he'd suffer the fate of many of his predecessors. He'd fall.

Over the course of two days, Logan had discovered

the news that Scott had raped and beaten the wrong girl. He'd gotten the bartender's twin sister instead, the one Sadie had been after for her house. This news he got from Mark Tanner, who claimed that he had one of Honey's girls wrapped around his finger — or some other digit.

After thinking it over, Logan decided to let the right girl, the bartender, go unpunished for a while. From what he'd heard she had suffered along with her sister, anyway. If things didn't go his way, he could always see to it that she got what was coming to her. Right now he was content to wait a while and see how his harassment tactics — engineered by his men under Tanner's direction — fared.

He left his office as evening came and hurried to his rooms, where he knew Angela Pettibone was waiting. He had seen the blonde stranger around town a few times and now she, along with Honey O'Day herself, had become a fantasy for him to enjoy while he was with Angela. In fact, more and more of late he was enjoying the fantasy more than the woman he was with.

It was definitely time for a change.

It was for the third night that Tanner had planned the initial act of vandalism for Honey's Place. The men he trusted to handle it were Sam Gates and Fred Masters. What he didn't know was that Mike Early and Alex Pennell would also be present.

The visit was Pennell's idea.

"I've heard they've got a gorgeous blonde that just sits up on a platform all night and watches."

"What's the attraction there?" Early asked.

"I just want to see her," Pennell said. "Maybe she gets lonely while she's up there. Maybe she'll want some company tonight."

"Tanner's got something planned for tonight, Alex," Early said. "He's sending Gates and Masters in."

"We're not gonna get in their way," Pennell said. "Come on, Mike, a quick look. I've got to see if she's as beautiful as everybody says she is."

"Compared to who?" Early asked. "Big Zelda?"

"That's unkind, Mike," Pennell said, sounding wounded. "I told you, I was just curious. To tell you the truth, she did taste a little fatty."

Early shook his head and said, "Come on. We'll have a beer and then leave. There's other places in town."

"Like Sadie's," Pennell said, with enthusiasm.

"For you," Early said, and they started walking towards Honey's Place with Pennell regaling him with the good points of Sadie's House.

Early was letting the words slide right past him, because he was thinking about the blonde on the platform. He'd heard about her too, that she just sat and watched with a rifle over her knees.

Could it be the same one? He'd been resisting the urge to go and find that woman ever since he saw her ride into town and, according to the liveryman, her horse was still there.

Maybe this was the night to finally get it done, and then maybe he'd be free of her presence in his dreams, both day and night.

Mark Tanner positioned himself across the street for two reasons. One was to be around when the fun started and to make sure it went off as planned.

Number two was just in case the sheriff or his deputies decided to act like real lawmen. If they did, he'd remind them whose payroll they were on.

When Tanner saw Gates and Masters pass through the batwing doors he smiled confidently. They were probably his two best men. They were competent and, above all, they did whatever he told them to do without question.

He was thinking about the next time he would have his woman, the one who worked in Honey's Place, when he was startled from his reverie by the appearance of Mike Early and Alex Pennell.

As *they* entered through the batwing doors he thought angrily, "What the hell were they doing there?"

If they messed things up, they'd have to answer to him even before they answered to Logan, because before Logan called them on the carpet, he'd take it out on Tanner . . . and Mark Tanner didn't intend for that to happen.

CHAPTER TEN

Liz saw the two pairs of men enter, scant moments apart, and was hard put at that point to tell which two had the mischief in mind. As the second pair entered, however, Honey O'Day worked her way across the room to Liz's platform and managed to catch her attention.

"The second pair," she said, pointing with her chin. "The one with the dark hair and big shoulders."

"What about him?"

"That's Mike Early."

Liz nodded and Honey drifted away, stopping here and there to say hello and goodbye to some of the more regular customers.

Liz took a second look at Mike Early who had walked with his friend or partner to the end of the bar. The other two men who had come in ahead of them were standing at the center of the bar.

On the subject of Mike Early, the man certainly did have a pair of shoulders on him, and traveling downward with her eyes she noticed that everything else seemed to be in proper proportion. On top of being built like some kind of Greek God from her childhood reading, the man also had a strong featured, handsome face. Liz felt her heart begin to pound just looking at him, and she tried to shake it off. Her only interest in him should have been as someone that might be able to help them.

She looked closer at the first two men who had entered, and saw that they were two typical hardcases. They were the type of men a man like Ed Logan would hire, not caring what they did for money as long as they got it. That much showed in their faces.

The man with Early was harder to figure. He had an open, pleasant face and bantered with the girls — Lori behind the bar, and Sandy as she circulated — but at the same time she could see him fitting in with the other two, and not quite fitting in with Mike Early.

Early was the sore thumb and, annoyingly, as her eyes swept over the room for hints of trouble, she found herself always finishing off on him, but if he noticed her at all, he gave no sign. Many of the men in the room were looking up at her, either out of admiration or open curiousity, but Early seemed to have neither.

It was while she was looking at Mike Early that the

trouble started, and her carelessness — picking that particular moment to be more woman than "Angel Eyes" — could have been costly. As it ended up, it cost Honey some furnishings.

"Damn you, Gates, I was talking to her first," one man yelled. The "her" he was talking about was Katrina, which did not surprise Liz in the least. What did surprise her was how fast things got out of hand.

From her vantage point high above the floor she saw the man suddenly pick up a nearby chair and swing it at the man he'd called Gates. The second man sidestepped in what appeared to be a practiced motion, and the chair slid from the first man's grasp — seemingly by accident — and sailed over the bar, smashing into the mirror behind it. The mirror shattered loudly, shards of glass flying every which way and knocking liquor bottles onto the floor from the shelves beneath. The man called Gates picked up a chair then and held it high over his head. Liz fired a shot that passed close enough by his ear for him to feel the breeze.

All eyes swung upward and they saw Liz standing on her feet, her rifle pointing right at the man with the chair.

"Stand just like that, mister," she called out, "don't move a muscle. I think we'll take bets on how long it takes you to get tired and finally drop that chair."

"Hey, what is this?" he said. He started to lower the chair and she fired another shot. It passed him by and lodged with the other bullet in the wall where the mirror used to be. Immediately his arms straightened, and he held the chair over his head.

"He started it," he shouted, indicating the other man.

"And I'm finishing it," Liz said. She turned her attention to the other man and said, "What's your name, friend?"

"Masters," the man replied, grudgingly.

"Well, Mr. Masters, it looks like you broke some glass."

"So?"

The man's hand hovered perilously close to his gun as if he was undecided about drawing it.

"You draw that gun, mister, and I'll put a hole clean through you."

His hand stiffened for a moment and then relaxed.

"Now you're going to have to pay for that mirror and for whatever liquor bottles you broke, not to mention the chair. Is that chair broke, Lori?"

Lori held up a piece of splintered chair leg and said, "Busted up good."

The man stared at the space where the mirror used to be, then looked back at Liz.

"I ain't got enough money to pay for that."

"Well, that's okay," Liz assured him. "Just take out whatever money you do have and lay it on the bar."

"What?"

"I think you heard me," she said. "Don't make me shoot off an earlobe just to test your hearing."

The man almost put his hand to his earlobe, but

stopped short of the embarrassing move. Instead he dug into his pocket — which was embarrassing enough — and began to draw out his money. Meanwhile, the other man was starting to sweat, and his arms were aching.

"Mr. Gates, if you drop that chair before I tell you to, I'm going to put a hole through your right foot."

"It's getting heavy," he complained.

"You should have thought of that before you picked it up."

The other man had finally stopped pulling coins and paper money from his pocket and was standing there waiting to see what was going to come next.

"Honey? Collect the man's money, count it out, then write out an I.O.U. for the rest of it, from him to you."

Honey did as she was told, counted the money and prepared the I.O.U.

"Now give it to him to sign."

"I ain't signing nothing."

"Yes, you are," Liz said, "that is, if you want to keep your fingers. I can shoot them off from here, you know. I've done it before."

The man looked down at his hands, flexed his fingers, then cursed and picked up the pencil Honey had laid at his elbow. He hastily scribbled his name on the I.O.U. and dropped the pencil to the bartop.

"Hey, Lady," Gates shouted, "I'm going to drop — "

"If you drop it and it breaks, you'll have to pay for it."

"Well, what else can I — "

"Why don't you just put it down?"

"Can I?"

"Sure," Liz said. "You look ridiculous standing there like that."

Everyone began to laugh then as Gates put the chair down with a bang, and Masters glared at Liz.

After the laughter had died down she told them, "Now you fellas run along like good boys and cause your trouble somewhere else. If you come back here again, I'm afraid I'll have to spank you both."

Again the place erupted in laughter as the two men slowly moved towards the door.

People began to mill about now that the excitement was over, and even though Liz was trying to keep an eye on the two men until they were out the door, her view was partially blocked.

Masters, feeling that he had been the more embarrassed of the two, decided he was going to shoot the lady off her perch. On top of vindicating himself he felt he'd probably get a medal from Ed Logan.

As he started to draw his gun Liz saw the move, but there was someone blocking her aim and she didn't want to hit an innocent bystander. She watched as the man brought his gun up, waiting in vain for an opening, and then suddenly there was Mike Early. He closed one big hand around the man's bicep and squeezed until the man dropped his gun, then took hold of the back of the man's pants and ran him towards the door and out onto the street. He turned to look at

Gates, who backed off and fled through the doors under his own power.

"Excitement's over, folks," Honey called out. She slapped her hand over the money that was still on the bar and said, "The fella that just went out of here by the seat of his pants is buying!"

CHAPTER ELEVEN

Liz climbed down from her platform and caught Rita's attention.

"Get Willie for me, will you?"

"Sure, Liz."

When Willie arrived Liz shoved her rifle into his hands, surprising him.

"What am I supposed to do with this?"

"Climb up there and look mean. I'll be back in a little while."

"Up there? Me?"

"Go ahead," she said, "you'll be fine. I'll still be in the room."

"All right!" he said, and eagerly scampered up the ladder to sit in her seat, rifle ready. He assumed an expression he obviously thought was "mean", and Liz hoped that no one would end up laughing themselves to death.

From across the room Honey gave her a question-
ing look, and Liz answered it by looking over at Mike
Early who was in earnest conversation with his com-
panion. Honey nodded, and Liz started to work her
way across the room to where Early was.

"You must be crazy!" Alex Pennell had told Mike
Early after Early had kept Masters from shooting the
woman on the platform. That remark led to their
"earnest conversation" during which Early assured
him that he had done nothing wrong.

"Nothing wrong? You were the one who warned
me that they'd be here. We weren't supposed to do
anything to interfere with them."

"Masters was making a mistake," Early said with
conviction.

"Sure, tell that to Tanner," Pennell said, "tell that
to Logan, tell them . . . uh oh. . . ."

Pennell broke off and stared past Early, and the big
man turned to see what he was staring at. He couldn't
blame Pennell for staring when he saw what or who it
was.

From a distance Liz Archer was beautiful, but as
she closed the gap between them she became more
and more stunning.

"Hi," she said.

"Hello."

"I want to buy you a drink and thank you for what
you did."

Early didn't need the prodding of Pennell's elbow
in his back to say, "Sure."

"Shall we sit at a table?"

Early looked the packed saloon over and said, "I
don't see any open tables."

"There's one towards the back," Liz said. "Follow me."

Pennell made a great show of clearing his throat, and Liz looked at him.

"What's wrong with your friend?"

"He's got something stuck in his throat," Early said. "He's just leaving."

Pennell glared at Mike Early's back as Early followed Liz through the crowd, then turned to Lori and ordered another drink.

"You like men, honey?" he asked her while she was pouring.

"I can take them or leave them," Lori said, and walked away.

"That figures," Pennell muttered to himself.

The table Liz took Mike Early to was Honey O'Day's table, which was always open. They sat down and Liz beckoned Sandy over.

"What can I do for you?" Sandy asked, smiling broadly at Mike Early. The smile wilted somewhat when she realized that he only had eyes for Liz.

"Can you bring us a couple of beers, Sandy?" Liz asked.

"Sure, hon, right away."

"You carry some weight here, for someone who just got to town a few days ago," Early said.

"Oh? You saw me ride in?"

"Everybody saw you ride in, lady," Early said. "You have a way of attracting attention."

Sandy returned with the beers, set them down, tried her smile on Early again, then shrugged and left them alone.

"What's your name?" he asked.

"Liz Archer," she said, "and you're Mike Early."

"And you didn't just bring me over here to buy me a drink. What's on your mind?"

Liz stared at him over the rim of her beer mug and said, "You work for Ed Logan."

"That's right."

"Why?"

Early considered the question for a few moments before answering.

"He's got a lot of money," he finally said, "and I figure I can follow him around for awhile and pick up whatever drops out of his pockets."

"For awhile?"

"Yeah, for awhile."

"And then what?"

"And then move on."

"Does that mean you don't have any sort of loyalty to Logan? You don't feel obligated to him?"

"My only loyalty, and my only obligation, is to myself, Miss Archer."

"Liz," she replied. "Since we're going to be working together, you can call me Liz."

"*We* are going to be working together?" he asked, raising his dark, perfectly shaped eyebrows. His cheekbones were perfect, too. High and strong, hollowing his cheeks out before they flared out to a solid jaw. Most of the time Liz watched people's eyes when she was talking to them, but in Mike Early's case she watched his mouth. She couldn't help but wonder what it would feel like to have that mouth kissing her, or sliding over her body . . .

"You're going to work for Logan?" he asked.

"He hasn't offered," Liz said, "and if he did, I wouldn't accept. No, that's not what I meant."

"Then what did you mean?"

"I'm authorized to offer you a job here at Honey's Place."

"Doing what?"

"Helping to keep it out of Ed Logan's hands."

"For what pay?"

"Oh, probably nothing like what you're getting from Ed Logan."

"Then why should I change sides?"

She leaned forward and said, "Because it's the right thing to do."

"What else can you offer me?"

"Well, I'd have to talk to Honey . . ."

"No," he said, "not Honey, *you*. What can *you* offer me that would make me change sides?"

She stared at him and then said, "What did you have in mind?"

"What I have in mind is you," Mike Early said, surprising himself with his own boldness, but then this woman was pretty bold, and he wanted to keep her interest.

"Me? Where?"

"In my bed."

"And that would make you take the job?"

He thought it over for a few seconds and then said, "Yeah," as if it surprised even him. "Yeah, that would do it."

Liz took a deep breath and just stared at him, dreading what she had to say next.

"Then I guess we don't have a deal."

"What?"

"I'm not a whore, Mike," Liz said, "if I was I'd be working over at Sadie's."

"I didn't mean . . . "

"So if that's your price," she said, driving right past his protests, "I'm afraid I can't pay it."

"I don't . . ."

"Of course," she went on, "that doesn't mean we can't go to bed together." ‾

"I want to . . . what? What did you say?"

"I said I want to go to bed with you."

With a great deal of satisfaction she could see that she had thrown him off balance.

"But you just said . . ."

"I said I wouldn't go to bed with you to get you to work for Honey," Liz said. "I would however, go to bed with you for my own pleasure."

What was she up to, Early wondered. Was she telling the truth or was she planning something?

"When?"

"After we close."

"And it has nothing to do with the offer you just made me on behalf of Honey O'Day."

"Nothing."

"What is she going to say about that?"

"What can she say? A girl has to have her fun too, doesn't she?"

"All right," Early said. "Where?"

"I'm afraid it will have to be your room," she said. "Mine's upstairs and I can't get you in here after closing."

"All right," he said. "I have a room in the hotel at the south end of town."

"Fine," she said. "I'll meet you there."

Mike Early waited for something else, but when there was nothing forthcoming he stood up, feeling slightly weak in the legs.

"Until later, then."

"I'm looking forward to it," she said and watching him walk away, she realized just how much she was looking forward to it.

It made *her* slightly weak in the knees.

Outside of Honey's Place Pennell asked Early, "What did she want?"

"Just what she said," Early answered, "to buy me a drink for helping her out."

"Yeah, well Tanner ain't gonna buy you a drink and neither is Logan. What are you going to tell them?"

"The same thing I told you. Masters was making a big mistake."

"I don't think they'll agree with you."

"I think they will."

"What are you going to do now?"

"I think I'll go back to my room."

"Good. Think about what you're going to tell them tomorrow. I'm going over to Sadie's. She's got a new chinee gal that I want to try."

"I'll see you tomorrow, then."

"It better be before you see Logan," Pennell advised, "because I doubt you'll be seeing anyone after that."

Early simply said, "Good night, Alex," and headed for his hotel to prepare his reception for Liz Archer.

After Early and his friend left, Honey came over and sat with Liz.

"What did he say?"

"He didn't say yes and he didn't say no."

"What, then?"

Liz stood up and said, "The matter is still open for discussion."

"Maybe I should talk to him myself."

"Tomorrow," Liz said, "talk to him tomorrow."

"All right."

"I have to relieve Willie before he falls off," Liz said, looking up at the boy who was craning his neck, apparently trying to see if there was anyone underneath the platform.

As Early reached his hotel two figures stepped out of the shadows cast by the streetlamp.

Gates and Masters.

"We've been waiting for you," Early," Masters said.

Masters and Gates had talked about getting even with the blonde on the platform after they'd left Honey's Place, but they also wanted to get even with Mike Early. Masters especially wanted a piece of Early because when he'd checked his arm where the big man had grabbed him he saw bruises in the shape of fingers.

The man had marked him and, by God, he was going to do some marking of his own.

In addition, Tanner had grabbed ahold of him after

they'd left — or been thrown out of — Honey's Place, and it had embarrassed them to tell their story, which Tanner said he'd take to Logan.

They had to get some self-respect back, and the only way they could think to do it was to hurt Mike Early, and hurt him bad.

"I'm sleepy, boys," Early said. "Let's talk tomorrow."

"We ain't here to talk," Gates said.

"We're here to pay you back for sticking your nose where it didn't belong and for siding with that blonde bitch."

"Why don't we wait and hear what Logan thinks about what happened, huh? Let's not go off half-cocked . . ."

"I'll give you half-cocked," Masters said.

It was unfortunate for the two men that they decided to hurt Early with their hands rather than with their guns. As Masters stepped towards him Early simply stepped back and kicked him in the balls. The man gagged and dropped to the ground, curling up into a fetal position, fighting for breath.

"Damn you . . ." Gates said, and now he started to draw his gun.

Early quickly closed the distance between them and clamped his hand over the man's gunhand. He exerted pressure and said, "Drop it or I'll crush every bone in your hand."

Gates tried to resist, but Early was too strong and he finally dropped his gun. Instead of easing up, however, Early kept the pressure on, squeezing the man's hand into a fist and then continuing to squeeze until Gates was driven to his knees by the pain, tears streaming from his eyes.

Finally, mercifully, Early released Gates's hand and the man clutched it to his body like a wounded bird.

"I'll see you boys in Logan's office, bright and early tomorrow morning. 'Night, now."

CHAPTER TWELVE

Everything Liz had thought about Mike Early was true, and more.

She was seated atop him, the length of him fitted snugly inside of her, and she was riding him gently, rocking up and down as if they were on a boat and she were moving with the motion of the water. He in turn was palming her breasts, squeezing her nipples and every so often pulling her towards him so that he could suck them. She had her hands pressed flat against his chest, which was as hard as a rock.

This was their second time.

The first had come after Honey had closed her place down for the night. Liz had wrangled a key out of her for the back door and told her she'd be back late. Honey was plainly curious, but did not ask any questions.

When Liz reached Mike Early's hotel she'd wondered if he'd really be waiting for her. If he wasn't, that would be fine, and if he was . . . well, that would be *just* fine.

She shook the desk clerk awake and said, "Mike Early's room?"

The clerk gaped at her with watery eyes, then swallowed hard and said, "Room sixteen, top of the stairs and end of the hall."

"Thanks."

She climbed the stairs, found room sixteen at the end of the hall as promised, and knocked.

"Come in," Early's voice called.

Liz admitted to a certain amount of anticipation as she turned the doorknob to enter. Aside from any further conversation about saving Honey's Place, this promised to be a very interesting night.

She pushed the door open and saw that there was very little light in the room. The lamp on the wall was turned way down low and she entered cautiously.

"So you came."

It was only when he spoke that she located him, seated on the bed.

"I said I would. Don't tell me you didn't believe me?"

"Let's just say I was . . . wary."

"Suspicious is more like it, if you ask me," Liz said. "What did you think I was going to do, bring some help to persuade you to work for Honey O'Day?"

"The thought had entered my mind."

"Well, at this very moment, Mike Early, I don't care if you work for her or not."

Liz slammed the door shut behind her for emphasis.

"And if you don't mind, I'm going to turn up the light so I can see."

"Why?"

"For all I know you may have some help hidden in here someplace."

"Am I going to need help?"

"Oh, no, I'm here quite willingly, and we both know why."

"Go ahead, turn up the lamp."

She adjusted the lamp up to about halfway and then turned to look at him. He was sitting on the bed wearing his pants, but no shirt or boots. Hanging on the bedpost was his gun, within easy reach.

"If you don't mind," she said, unbuckling her gunbelt and walking towards him, "I'll hang mine on the other side."

As she did so he asked, "Isn't it a little odd for a woman to be walking around wearing a gun?"

"You mean it's odd not to see me in a dress in some saloon, or some man's kitchen? I'm not like other women, Mike."

"I've managed to guess that."

She hung her gun over the bedpost and then started to unbutton her shirt. As she stripped it off he saw that she was wearing nothing underneath it, and caught his breath when her breasts came into view. She turned her back to him so she could sit down and pull her boots off, giving him an unobstructed view of her back. Then she stood up and turned back to him.

"All right," she said, "we're on even terms. It's your move."

Mike Early had not been with as many women as say, an Alex Pennell, but he'd been with his fair share, and it was his opinion that Liz Archer had the most magnificent breasts he'd ever seen. They were large and firm, perfectly shaped, tipped with pink nipples which were already swelling beneath his eyes.

He stood up then in response to her words and removed his pants. She saw his erection outlined against the fabric of his underwear and felt a shiver go through her. He was large, larger than most, though by no means monstrously huge. He tugged the underwear down over his hips and dropped it to the floor. His engorged penis stood straight up from a thatch of thick, black hair. The crown — and that was the perfect word for it — was wonderfully shaped, a mixture of red and purple which seemed to grow deeper, and larger, as she stared at it.

"Your turn."

She nodded, licked her lips, and removed her own pants and underwear. Early's eyes grew wider when he saw the golden hair between her legs. He could actually smell her readiness in the air of the room. Suddenly, his cock began to ache and pulse.

She put one knee on the bed and he did the same. Suddenly they were closer, only inches away from each other. Each was acutely aware of the heat of the other's body. Liz made the first move because she couldn't wait. She reached out and ran her nails over the length of him, then closed her hand around him, letting the spongy head stick out.

Early reached for her breasts and let the undersides

rest in his hands, as if testing their weight. He brushed his thumbs over her nipples, which responded by tightening.

"Do you know what I was wondering while we were at Honey's?" Liz asked.

"What?"

"What your mouth would feel like . . ." she said, leaning over to kiss him fleetingly, licking his lips to taste them, and then finished, ". . . all over my body."

"Well," he said, gripping her breasts in his large hands, "we can answer that easily enough, can't we?"

He laid her down on the bed and she spread her legs comfortably. He started with her face, running his lips over her brow, her nose, kissing her briefly, and then running his tongue from her chin to her breasts. She shivered when he encountered her nipples, tugging on them easily with his lips, wetting them with his tongue, and then scraping them with his teeth. She thought she was going to come immediately, but she didn't quite make it.

He continued on his way, then, moving from her stomach, pausing to stick his tongue in her naval, and she watched as he dipped lower, running his tongue ever so lightly over the lips of her vagina so that she clenched her buttocks waiting for him to plunge deeper. He did not, however. He simply moved on and she remembered that she had told him "all" of her body, and that was what he intended to do.

He kissed her thighs, her knees, her shins and finally her feet, actually sucking her toes. This, for reasons totally unknown to either of them, excited them tremendously.

"Turn over," he said, and she obeyed. He kissed her ankles, ran his tongue over her calves, over the hollows behind her knees — which made her pussy ache, for some reason — the backs of her thighs, and then he lingered on her buttocks.

Early was almost as impressed with her ass as he had been with her breasts. He wanted to linger over it, but had other ground to cover, so he vowed to return and continued on. With his tongue he traced the line of her spine until he got between her shoulder blades, and then he kissed them. He kissed her rounded shoulders, and then tongued the nape of her neck. He was enjoying himself immensely because he'd never "travelled" over a woman's body so fully before, and this was easily the most beautiful, most desirable body he'd ever encountered.

She started to turn over then and he said, "Don't."

"I can't . . ." she started. She wanted to tell him that she couldn't stand it anymore, but suddenly he was running his tongue down that crack between the cheeks of her behind, and then his big hands were kneading her and she moaned as he pressed and squeezed her ass. A finger slid between her thighs from behind and probed until it found her juicy center, and then it entered and she groaned aloud.

"Turn over," he said hoarsely, "I can't wait anymore."

"That's what I was trying to tell . . ." she began, but he was on her then — actually on top of her, full length — and his mouth was on hers, his tongue was in her mouth, exploring. She caught it between her teeth and held it for a second, then sucked on it as he pressed his hairy chest against her breasts, flattening them and chafing her nipples. She could feel the length of him between them, hot and pulsing, and with her hands she maneuvered his hips over her, then took hold of him and guided him into her.

As the head of his penis slid past her wet entrance he suddenly thrust himself into her, piercing her fully. A cry caught in her throat, and he moaned as suddenly they were bouncing on the bed in perfect unison. Everytime their hips came together with an audible slap they both moaned at the maximum penetration they were achieving together.

They strove on, faster and faster, until she felt a rush in her legs, felt his body tense and then almost drowned out his roar with a cry of her own as they both reached the pinnacle together.

That was the first time.

This was the second.

This one had started playfully. They had begun to wrestle and he had allowed her to push him onto his back and straddle him. From there she had crawled up his chest and settled down with her pussy over his face. He had gone to work with his tongue, licking her, sucking her, until sitting there on his face she had an enormous orgasm.

She had laid full length on him to rest, and then she sat up and straddled him again.

She rode him slowly, allowing his length to almost fully leave her, then sliding down him again, slowly, inch by inch, until he was fully inside her again. His lips were on her nipples, and she closed her eyes as he sucked. She was running her hands all over his body, wherever she could reach, and at one point she reached behind her to cup his sack and caress it gently. In that position her back was arched and her breasts were thrust forward. Early revelled in the sight of her, the smell of her, the small touches, and it was he who increased the tempo. She caught on immediately and complied, riding him faster, bracing her hands against his sternum and before long they were each wracked by another orgasm, as great or greater than the first.

CHAPTER THIRTEEN

"You sound pretty educated," she said later, held in the circle of his strong arms.

"You sound fairly educated, yourself."

"I read some as a child, try to read a bit now."

"I used to be — are you ready — a school teacher in the East."

"Really? What happened?"

"I got tired of the little brats, so I came out West."

"Did you fit in?"

"I didn't, at first, but I learned."

"Where did you learn to do what we just did?"

"Some of that I've never done before," he admitted.

"Neither have I. It seemed natural, though, don't you think?"

"Yes, I do think. I've also been thinking about your offer —"

"Don't," she said, cutting him off.

"But I want to tell you that I think I —"

"Don't talk about that, Mike," she said. "It'll spoil everything. That's between you and Honey. I told her I'd ask you once, and I asked you."

"Why did she ask you to ask me?" he said. "We've never met before."

"I think she thought we'd . . . get along."

"And we have."

She pushed herself up to a seated position and said to him, "Then let's keep it that way. Let's not talk about any of that."

He studied her for a few moments, and she knew he was wondering if she was sincere. She knew she was — she'd enjoyed herself too much not to be — but it remained for him to make up his own mind.

"All right, we won't."

"And now it's my turn."

"To do what?"

Her eyes seemed to shine, and she showed him.

She began a slow inspection of his body, using her mouth, her tongue, and her teeth. Starting as he had, she worked her way over his torso, nipping his nipples hard enough to make him jump. She traced a path through the hair on his chest, tasting the perspiration that they had already worked up, and not finding it unpleasant at all. Her tongue glided over his belly and through the tangle of pubic hair until she was presented with his rigid erection.

She didn't have his will power, however. When her exploration reached his swollen organ the sight of it, combined with the scent his body was giving off made it so she couldn't resist. She just couldn't pass it up with a vow to return. She took him in her mouth and suckled him lovingly, cradling his testicles in one hand and encircling his base with the other. She moaned as she sucked him to incredible fullness. She played with the head a while, allowing it to pop in and out of her mouth while she stroked his length with one hand, and then she took him into her mouth as fully as she could without gagging. She began to suck harder then, bobbing her head up and down, using her hands as well until finally, unable to hold back any longer he cried out and ejaculated into her mouth. Incredibly he had a lucid thought even when it felt as if his head was going through the roof.

It was his turn next, and what could he possibly do to top this?

Liz left rather than spend the night, so they could both have time to think.

Early had expected some kind of trick from her, and what he seemed to have gotten was a beautiful young woman who enjoyed sex — sex with *him* — and was apparently sincere about not using her body to woo him over to her side in the Honey's Place dispute.

Even if she hadn't come to him, however, he'd already made his decision, and it really had nothing to do with her.

Well, not much, anyway.

Liz was a little confused, but she was confusing herself.

Had she really gone to Mike Early's hotel with no

intention of trying to use her body to sway him to Honey's side? She was pretty sure she had. She'd gotten that pit of the stomach feeling when Honey pointed him out to her, and she honestly thought that from that moment on she knew she'd end up in bed with him, no matter what his position was in the Honey's Place dispute.

By the time she got back to her room she was convinced that she'd only gone to his room for some enjoyable sex.

She was also pretty sure that when Honey approached him the next day, he'd come over to their side.

So, if her body had swayed him even though she hadn't meant it to, did it count the same as using her body to buy him?

It was confusing.

Of course there was always the chance that he *wouldn't* come over to their side, and that she was just flattering herself.

She'd find out tomorrow.

CHAPTER FOURTEEN

In the morning Liz came downstairs and discovered that working for Honey meant breakfast on the house. Almost the entire crew was in residence, seated at three tables, and it was Belle who was doing the cooking.

"What will you have?" Belle asked, drying her hands on the apron around her waist.

"What have you got?"

"Steak, eggs, spuds, biscuits, coffee . . ."

"Sounds fine."

"Coming up."

Liz looked around and found that there was an open chair next to Honey, and one next to Lori at another table. She decided to sit next to Lori because she didn't want to answer any questions about her and Mike Early. Not yet, anyway.

"How do you girls keep your figures with breakfasts like these?" Liz asked, sitting down next to Lori. Also at the table were Sandy and Rita.

"We alternate cooking," Lori explained, "and Belle happens to be the best cook."

"On Belle's days," Sandy said, "we eat breakfast and nothing else the rest of the day.

"Speak for yourself," Rita said.

"Except for Rita," Sandy went on, "who thinks there should be four meals a day, and twice as many on Sunday."

"So I like to eat," Rita said. "Men like chunky girls as much as skinny ones."

"I'm not skinny, chile," Sandy said, "I'm slim."

"You're both lovely," Lori said, "so let's not fight."

Both girls looked at her and Sandy said, "We're not fightin', honey."

"You're so serious, Lori," Rita chided her.

"I guess so," Lori said, looking down into her dish.

"How's Lisa?" Liz asked.

"She's much better," Lori said. "The bruises are fading and she can speak clearly now. She's so lucky that none of her teeth were broken. I'm going to take her a plate as soon as I finish."

"Good," Liz said. "I'm glad to hear she's feeling better."

At that moment Belle came out with two plates and placed one in front of Liz. The other one was obviously hers and she sat at Honey's table to eat it.

It was only when Trina appeared on the stairs that

Liz realized that Lisa and Trina were the only ones missing.

"Where's mine?" she asked Belle.

"On the stove," Belle said sweetly. "Gotta get down here a lot earlier if you want to be served, dear."

Trina ignored the gibe and went to get her own breakfast. When she returned she sat at a table by herself.

Liz sampled Belle's breakfast and found it delicious. She was going to have to warn Honey not to expect her to take a turn cooking, or most of her girls would quit on her.

While Liz was enjoying breakfast, Mike Early was wondering if he should have his before or after seeing Ed Logan. If he had it before he'd be anticipating the meeting, and if he had it after he'd have a bad taste in his mouth. Either way the meal was ruined, so he headed for Logan's office knowing that the man always came in early.

He knocked and entered in response to Logan's voice. The town boss was alone in the room.

"They were here," Logan said. He was seated behind his desk. "Gates, Masters *and* Tanner. I sent them away."

Maybe it wouldn't be as distasteful as he thought if he didn't have to see Gates and Masters.

"Sit down, Early," Logan said. "I'm a reasonable man. I'd like to hear your side of it."

"Of what?"

"Of what happened last night."

"Since I don't know what they told you happened last night," Early said, "I can only say that I stopped Masters and Gates from making a stupid mistake."

"Which would have been?"

"Killing Liz Archer."

"And who is Liz Archer?"

"The girl on the platform."

"Oh yes, I'd heard about her even before last night's unfortunate incident. Why would it have been a bad idea for them to kill her?"

"Because you don't need that kind of attention right now. That's something that Gates and Masters are incapable of understanding. You don't just go around shooting people. It attracts unwanted attention."

"And Tanner?"

"If Tanner had been there he would have stopped them, too."

"So they lied then?"

"What did they say?"

"That you sided with this Liz Archer against them. That you're working for Honey O'Day now."

"Yeah, they lied — but I have had an offer."

"What kind of offer?"

"To work for Honey O'Day. To try and keep you from taking over her place."

"And what was your answer."

"I said I'd think it over."

"And have you? No, wait, don't answer that." Logan remained silent for a moment, staring down at his desk top, then looked up at Early again.

"You seem to be a smart man, Early, so you'll understand when I tell you to accept this offer."

"You want me to go to work for her, while still working for you?"

"Right. It will help me to have a man — my man — on the inside. What do you say?"

"For the same pay?"

"You'll be getting paid by me and by Honey O'Day," Logan pointed out. "And with all the women she's got working for her, think of the fringe benefits."

The man's leer offended Early.

"I'd still like a little more money."

"All right," Logan said, "I'm a fair man. I'll give you another fifty dollars a month. That makes an even hundred."

"These buffoons you have working for you, like Gates and Masters, they think fifty a month is pretty good."

"And you don't? You don't think a *hundred* a month is pretty good?"

"I think five hundred a month is a lot better."

Logan blinked and said, "Isn't that a lot of money?"

"You have a lot of money, Mr. Logan," Early said. "You tell me, is five hundred a lot of money?"

"What am I getting for it?"

"A brain," Early said, "which is more than what you're getting from all of the others combined."

Logan stared at the man for a moment, then smiled and said, "I like you, Early."

"But will you pay me?"

"I'll give you four hundred a month," Logan said, "and if I have Honey O'Day's place by the end of this month, you'll get a bonus. That's the best offer I have. Take it or leave it."

Early thought it over a moment trying to decide if he should negotiate the bonus now, but decided not to push it.

"Mr. Logan, you've got a deal."

CHAPTER FIFTEEN

Later that night Early walked into Honey's Place alone. From her platform Liz saw him, but he didn't look up at her. He searched the room, found who he was looking for, and walked over to Honey O'Day.

"Can we talk?"

She turned and looked at him — admiring him — and then said, "Sure."

"In your office?"

"Follow me."

Honey led him to her office, opened the door to let him in, then closed it and sat behind her desk.

"Liz Archer made me an offer which I understand was on your behalf," Early said.

"It was," she said, confirming it. "I understand that you're thinking it over."

"I'm considering it," Early replied in a noncommittal tone. "We didn't talk money."

"I can't pay you what Logan is paying you, that's obvious," Honey said.

"Make the offer."

She shrugged and said, "Fifty dollars a month, and that's stretching my payroll."

"I'll tell you what," Early said. "I'll do it for nothing."

"For nothing?" Honey asked, and then laughed. "Mister, I didn't get to be as old as I am by taking something for nothing every time it was offered to me. What's the catch?"

"No catch," he said. "If we manage to stave off Logan, or get rid of him, I'll expect a bonus."

"And just what kind of a bonus did you have in mind?"

"A piece of this place."

Her instinct was to say no, but she stopped and considered it.

"How big a piece?"

"Not as big as Logan wants."

"Is that all?"

He caught her eyes and held them.

"No, there could be . . . other considerations."

Honey O'Day felt something in the pit of her stomach she hadn't felt for a long time.

"Then you'll work for me?"

Early stood up, leaned over her desk so that his face was inches away from hers, and said, "I'll work *with* you, Honey. That'll be even better, don't you think?"

She felt his hand on her, and closed her eyes . . .

Liz saw Mike Early come out of Honey's office a full half-hour after they'd gone in. Honey wasn't with him. Early headed for the door, never looked her way, and left. She frowned. She didn't like being ignored, but then one night together didn't join them at the hip or anything.

Two could play at that game, anyway.

Mike Early went back to his hotel room to reflect on what he had done that day. In effect, he had changed his entire personality, because providence had suddenly dealt him a winning hand.

If he helped Ed Logan get Honey's Place away from Honey O'Day, he would end up with a big bonus above and beyond the four hundred a month.

If, on the other hand, Liz Archer and Honey O'Day — with a little help from him — managed to outlast Logan, he'd end up with a piece of Honey's Place, which he saw as a potential gold mine.

And then there were the women: Honey O'Day and her "staff" and, of course, Liz Archer.

Mike Early had changed an awful lot over the course of one day, but even he didn't know the true extent of this sudden personality change — or the consequences it would bring.

After closing Liz and Honey sat at the saloon owner's table together. Liz decided to ignore the fact that, when Honey had finally come out of her office after her talk with Mike Early, she'd seemed a little disheveled, and a little self-satisfied.

All of that meant nothing because Liz had gotten what she'd wanted, some bedtime with Mike Early.

True, she would have liked a repeat performance, but the jury wasn't quite out on that yet, either.

"Did you talk to Early?"

Honey hesitated and then said, "We talked."

"And?"

"He's . . . coming aboard," she said, keeping the details of the deal to herself for now.

"Well, good," Liz said, convinced that the woman was hiding something — something a lot more than a possible roll on her desktop with Mike Early. "I only hope he can help as much as you seem to feel he can."

"Before he left he said something about possibly bringing someone else in on it," Honey explained. "A couple of men on our side who aren't afraid of Ed Logan would be a big help." Honey gave Liz a funny look and asked, "Are you, uh, going out tonight?"

"No," Liz said, and then asked, "Are you?"

"No," Honey said, "not me."

"Well then, I guess we'd better get to bed," Liz said. "Tomorrow may be a big day for you."

"For us," Honey corrected. "Don't forget, you're part of this, too."

"I'm glad you remembered that . . ."

Someone did go out that night, though, and walked through the darkness to the north end of town where there was a rooming house owned by Ed Logan. It was used by many of his men, and one of them was waiting at the door for her.

"It's about time," Mark Tanner said. "Come on, I've been waiting twenty minutes."

"I'm sorry, Mark . . ." she said, but he grabbed

her by the arm and said, again, "Come on," pulling her into the house. He shut the door, locked it, and then pushed her along ahead of him until they reached his room. Tanner's room was on the first floor, while the rest of the men had second floor rooms.

When they were inside his room he lit a lamp and turned to her. She began to undress, unable to meet his stare. He watched with pleasure as her body came into view. Lovely smooth skin, long dark hair, small, round breasts.

"You said tonight you'd show me more," she said when she was totally naked.

"I will," he said, approaching her and putting a hand on her right breast. She closed her eyes, which he wrongly interpreted as a pleasurable reaction to his touch.

"You said you'd show me more tonight," Lori said, "more so that I could be like my sister."

"I will, Lori, I will, believe me," he said, cupping her chin with his other hand and squeezing until her face was misshapen, "but first talk to me, baby. Talk to me."

CHAPTER SIXTEEN

The next morning Ed Logan woke, sat up in bed, and looked down at the nude form of Angela Pettibone. He examined her critically and came to the conclusion that for a full-bodied woman of thirty-five or so she didn't look too bad. However, the fact that she simply "didn't look too bad" was enough to indicate, as other things had been doing from time to time, that it was time to change his "favorite."

He stood up, walked to the pump he'd had installed in his house and pumped out some water to wash with. Turning, he toweled himself off and stared at her ass. Was it beginning to spread, or was it his imagination?

He thought about Honey O'Day. The woman was even older than Angela, and was herself rather full-bodied, but God she was a classy looking woman who kept herself well, and that's what Ed Logan needed if he was going to get anywhere *outside* of Loganville, Wyoming. Logan had a huge political career ahead, and what he needed was not so much a wife or a lover as a hostess. Honey O'Day would certainly fit that bill much better than, say, an Angela Pettibone.

And then there was this Liz Archer. Physically she was superior to both Angela and Honey, and not just because she was ten to fifteen years younger. She was simply more beautiful than either of those women had ever been, more beautiful than any one woman had a right to be. She had obviously allied herself with Honey against him, but maybe if he talked with her, explained the facts of life to her, she'd come over to *his* side — in more ways than one.

He'd have to take care of that today, but there was something to be taken care of first.

Angela Pettibone, nee Petty, had turned over on her back and, lying that way, with her breasts flattened out and her legs spread, she had a slutty quality that gave him an instant reaction. The woman *was* simply marvelous in bed. There was absolutely nothing she wouldn't do, and so far he had no means of comparison with Honey or the Archer girl.

Still naked, his erection huge and throbbing, he walked to the bed, deciding that he'd keep Angela around for a while longer, just for situations like these, until he *did* have some means of comparison.

Her legs were spread so wide that her pinkness winked at him. He reached down between her legs and inserted one finger inside of her. She was already moist and instead of jumping in surprise, she simply opened her eyes and looked up at him, smiling.

Had the damned woman been awake the whole

time? Had she turned over in bed and posed for him, knowing what his reaction would be?

Did she know him that well?

No one should know him that well, he decided, and anyone who did had to be punished for it.

Angela had turned her head, craned her neck and, using one hand, had guided the head of his swollen cock to her mouth. She was laving the spongy head avidly with her tongue, making appreciative sounds deep in her throat. Her other hand strayed down to where his was, urging him to do more.

"Turn over, Angela, my dear," he said, removing his finger instead, "it's time for one of your spankings."

"Oh," she said, and then releasing her hold on him, she turned over to present her ample buttocks to him and added, "Good." She thrust her cheeks up high, accenting their roundness and revealing her anus and vagina to him.

His erection twitched when she said the word "good," in that tone of voice she had, and he began to wonder if her good qualities didn't outweigh her bad ones when she could elicit that response with one spoken word.

Of course, that too was a power which no one should be allowed to have over him.

This spanking, he decided, called for a belt.

That morning at breakfast Liz and Honey sat together, apart from the other women and Willie. Since Liz was using Willie, it was agreed that he could have breakfast with them. He was sitting with chunky

Rita who had taken to wearing very flimsy nighties around the boy, either to entice him or to tease him, and he was looking at her moon-eyed while they ate. She smiled at him from time to time, and Liz could see him shifting position in his chair to accomodate what must have been a very uncomfortable erection.

"There's something I didn't ask you when we talked last night," Liz said.

"What's that?"

"Is Early going to be staying here?"

"No, for more reasons than one."

"Well," Liz said, looking around her at the room-ful of lovely and desirable women, "some of them are obvious. What are the others?"

"We decided that it would be better if Logan didn't know that Mike . . . Early was on our side."

"Ah, sort of a double agent."

"What's that?"

"During the war there were men who pretended to work for one side while, in fact, they were working for the other. They were called double agents."

"That's interesting."

"And, if they were actually working for the first side after all, they were called triple agents."

Honey stared at Liz for a few moments and then said, "That's scary."

"And maybe something we should just be on the lookout for."

"You're right."

Liz could tell by the look on the other woman's face that she was berating herself. There was no need. She'd reacted to Mike Early as any woman would — as Liz herself had — and had temporarily lost her perspective. Hopefully she was back on the right track now.

"Where are Lisa and Lori this morning?"

"They're having breakfast in their room," Honey said. "They're doing that more and more these days, Liz. I'm starting to worry about those girls. The beating and rape of Lisa seems to have affected both of them and I can't say who's taking it harder."

"Would you like me to talk with them?"

"No," Honey said, and then hurriedly added, "Don't take offense, but if my girls have a problem, they know they can come to me. Let's just wait a while."

"You're the boss."

After breakfast there was a knock on the door and Willie answered it. It was just one of his new responsibilities.

He recognized the man at the door as one of Ed Logan's men.

"Whataya want?"

"I have a note for Miss Archer."

"Give it to me."

The man shook his head and said, "It's for Miss Archer and nobody else."

Willie turned and said, "Liz, there's a man here with a note for you."

Liz walked to the door and the man simply handed her a sealed white envelope and walked away.

"Lock the door, Willie," she said, turning to walk back to her table.

Willie obeyed, muttering under his breath, "I don't have to be told that."

"What is it?" Honey asked. "Personal?"

"Let's find out," Liz said, and broke it open.

Inside was a small piece of expensive stationery with a monogramed "E.L." on the top.

"That's Logan's stationery," Honey said.

Liz read the note and then passed it on to Honey.

"He wants to see you this morning, in his office, at your convenience." Honey frowned and looked at Liz. "What does he want with you?"

"That's fairly obvious," Liz said, taking the piece of paper back.

"Not to me."

"He wants to buy me off, Honey."

"Oh . . . yeah!" Honey frowned again and asked, "Are you going?"

"I'm going to hear what he has to say, yeah," she replied, "but he's not going to be able to buy me."

"Remember what we said about double agents," Honey said.

"I don't think I'm cut out for that kind of work," Liz said, dubiously, "but I'll keep it in mind."

CHAPTER SEVENTEEN

Liz went to Ed Logan's office in the afternoon preferring to make the man wait all morning. She knocked, and he called out for her to enter.

"Miss Archer?" he asked, rising.

She had seen him around town from a distance, and up close he was better looking — and older.

"That's right."

"I'm glad you could come. Please, sit down. Can I get you a drink?"

"Do you have any brandy?"

"I have some excellent brandy."

"Then I'll have some."

"As you wish."

Logan poured two brandies and handed her one. They each took a moment to study the other.

Liz saw a man in his early forties, well kept and attractive, with a certain amount of charm she was sure was a front. His hair and mustache were gray, and he was somewhat barrel-chested. He had a deep voice, one that would be a definite asset to a would be politician, and it was her experience that men who ran towns aspired to run something even larger.

What Ed Logan saw was a woman who was so beautiful as to be disconcerting this close. Looking at her, admiring her wide blue eyes, her golden hair, the full thrust of her breasts, he could almost forget for the moment that she was technically his enemy.

Unless he could convince her otherwise . . .

"No secretary," Liz said. "I'm surprised that a man of your stature doesn't have a secretary."

"I'm very capable of handling my business affairs on my own and don't see the need for one."

And, Liz thought, the less people who know about those business affairs, the better.

"Is that what I am?" she asked.

"What?"

"A business affair?"

She could see that he was studying her, trying to gauge what kind of comeback would be appropriate, and he apparently decided to play it straight.

"Well, what I have in mind *is* a business proposition, yes."

"I see."

"Shall I tell you what it is?"

"We'll never get anywhere if you don't."

"That's true," he said. "I understand that you've taken a job at Honey's Place, with Honey O'Day."

"That's right."

"You're a, uh, sort of watchdog?"

"Sort of."

"I also understand that you're very good at your job."

"You understand a lot," she said, "but I don't understand what you're getting at. I'm sure you can speak plainer that you have been so far, Mr. Logan."

"I wish you'd call me Ed."

"I'll stick with 'Mr. Logan' for the time being, if you don't mind."

"As you wish," he said with a shrug. "As for speaking plainer, it's quite simple, really. I'd like to hire you away from Honey O'Day."

"To do what?"

"Almost the same thing you're doing now," he said. "You see a man in my position — of my stature, as you put it — is fair game at all times."

"You want me to be your bodyguard?"

"That's exactly what I want."

"Mr. Logan, I'm very flattered," Liz said, putting her empty glass on the desk, "but you have a lot of men working for you."

"None of them are as lovely as you."

"I see." Liz paused, then said, "You want me to go where you go and watch your back at all times."

"Exactly."

"Does that include when you go to bed, when you take a bath, everything?"

"Well . . . yes."

"Were you hoping to make this relationship . . . personal, at all?"

"Well, I intend to pay you quite well to keep me alive. If something else should develop, I certainly wouldn't be adverse to having a woman as beautiful as you are . . ."

"I don't think I'm interested."

"And why not?"

"Because when I work for someone I expect them to be totally honest with me, and you are not, Mr. Logan."

As she said it she remembered just that morning, when Honey had obviously been keeping something from her about the deal she made with Mike Early.

"In what way am I being dishonest?"

"You don't want to hire me, Mr. Logan, you just want to get me away from Honey O'Day."

"Well, is that so bad?"

"It's not bad," Liz said, "It's just impossible."

"But you haven't heard my offer."

"And I don't want to. I think I'll be going."

"Wait!" he snapped, and not only was his voice different, but his entire manner had changed.

He was decidedly less formal.

"Listen, lady, what you're doing now is getting in my way. That's not a healthy thing for anyone to do, let alone a woman who thinks she's a man."

Now he was reverting to form, the veneer of the well-bred businessman gone. Logan was obviously another of those ambitious men who, had they channeled their ambitions in the right direction, probably could have gone far in earning high position and respect. Instead, they tried to demand respect through fear, instead of earning it.

"Well, you've finally gotten around to speaking plainer. You're also trying to bait me by insulting me, Logan," she said, dropping the "Mister," "but you can't insult me. You'd have to get on my level to do that, and you're just too far down the ladder."

"Listen . . ." he said, standing up so quickly that his desk moved.

"No, you listen. From what I understand you already own ninety percent of Loganville. Why do you have to go after Honey's Place, as well?"

"Because," he said, "ninety percent isn't the same as a hundred percent."

"You know, I've run into your kind before, Logan —"

"I don't think so," he said, interrupting her now. "I think when this whole thing is over you will have found it a very unique experience."

"I doubt it. Good afternoon, Mr. Logan."

"Bitch!" Logan hissed as she left.

He went to his window to watch her cross the street, his eyes on her perfect behind as it stretched the seat of her jeans. She *was* a true beauty.

It would be a shame to have to have her killed before he could have her.

CHAPTER EIGHTEEN

"He wanted you to be his what?" Honey O'Day asked in surprise.

"His bodyguard."

"What did you tell him?"

"What do you think I told him? I said I didn't want a job where I'd have to stoop that low."

Mike Early was also in Honey's office, and he chose that moment to speak up.

"You said that to Logan?"

"I did."

"That's the same as spitting in his face. Do you want to get yourself killed?"

"I have a penchant for the brutal truth."

"Uh-huh, and a penchant for trying to get yourself killed."

Honey O'Day, not as well-educated as Mike Early,

or as well-read as Liz Archer, asked, "What's a penchant?"

"A habit," Mike Early said, not taking his eyes off of Liz Archer, "and a bad one."

"Don't worry about it," Liz told Early.

"I worry about me, lady," he said, "you worry about yourself."

"It's a deal."

Honey looked back and forth from Early to Liz and thought that something was going on here that she couldn't see.

"What now?" she asked, the question being posed to either one of them.

Early deferred to Liz, who said, "We'll just have to wait until his next move — that is, unless we can find out in advance what it is."

"Maybe that can be arranged," Mike Early said, "given a little time."

"What about him finding out our moves?" Honey said. "Do you still think I've got a spy in my midst?"

"What's this?" Early asked.

"Liz thinks that there's someone here who is working for Logan."

"Any ideas who?" he asked, looking at Liz.

"No," Liz said, unwilling to mention her original suspicion of Trina. "Honey knows them a lot better than I do, and she can't hazard a guess."

"I just can't believe one of my girls would do that to me."

"Anybody will do anything to anyone," Mike Early said, "for a price."

"Does that include you?" Liz asked.

"Sometimes."

"What about this time?"

"I guess you'll just have to wait and see."

Liz thought that a sudden change had come over Mike Early. He didn't seem the same man she had shared a bed with the other night. Somehow, he'd gotten harder.

"Why did you take this job, Mike?"

"Didn't Honey tell you the terms of our agreement?"

"I didn't think it was necessary," Honey said, nervously. Was she worried about what Liz would think?

"I don't think it should be such a secret," Early said. "If I help to get Logan off her back, Honey's going to turn a piece of this place over to me." He looked at the older woman now and added, "We'll be partners."

Liz looked at Honey and asked, "How big a piece?"

"That's negotiable," Early said. He pushed away from the wall he'd been leaning on and said, "I can see you two have things to discuss. I'll get to work."

"What about that other man you mentioned?" Honey asked.

At the door Early said, "That's one of the things I'm going to work on."

After he left the two women faced each other over Honey's desk.

"Well, say something," Honey said, finally breaking the silence.

"You promised him a piece of this place?"

"A small piece."

"That remains to be seen, doesn't it?"

"You're not mad because I didn't offer you a piece, are you? It wasn't my idea, Liz, it was his. He said —"

"I don't want a piece of your place, Honey," Liz said, interrupting her.

"Then what's wrong?"

"You're fighting one man and you just turn around and hand your place to another. That doesn't make sense."

"If giving up a portion helps me keep the whole thing, then it does make sense."

"There are other ways."

"What ways? You tell me what other ways, Liz? Should I hire someone to kill Logan? A gunman?"

"No."

"Well then, it's my place and I'm doing my damnedest to keep it that way."

"All right, Honey. I can't fault you for that."

"All right."

Still, Liz couldn't help wondering if Honey wasn't just escaping from the lion into the mouth of the jackal.

Liz left Honey's office and started back to her room, wondering if she hadn't made a mistake by getting involved. Suddenly it was getting confusing, difficult to tell the good guys from the bad guys. Ed Logan was a bad guy of course, and their main objective was to foil his plans to take over the saloon, but after that who was who? Honey was a good guy, but what was Mike Early? And which of Honey's girls had suddenly decided to go over to the other side, and for what reason? Money? Fear? How about love?

Liz had to pass Lisa and Lori's room to get to hers, and as she did she heard loud voices coming from behind the door. She stopped to listen.

"This is crazy," one voice said.

"No, it's not crazy for me to want to be like you. I love you."

The two girls were *so* identical that it was impossible for Liz to tell who was speaking. She continued to listen, unable to put a label on the voice.

"But the price is too high!"

"I don't agree."

"Damn it — "

"Don't swear at me!"

"I don't mean to, but you make me so . . . crazy sometimes."

"I don't mean to." This voice sounded as if it were about to cry. "I was just trying to do what's best."

"And messing everything up as usual."

The reply was mumbled, and Liz suspected that this sister had dissolved into tears. She strained against the door, ear flat on the wood, hoping no one would come into the hallway at that moment.

"All right," she barely made out one voice saying, "it's all right. As usual I'll think of a way out."

After that they fell silent, and Liz continued on to her room.

Did the conversation she had just overheard mean that one of the twins was betraying Honey? And, if so, which one?

She went over the conversation again in her mind. It seemed that one sister had the misguided impression that by doing whatever she was doing, she was making herself more like her sister. Lisa had once been a whore, although Honey hadn't actually said that in so many words, and Lori was a good bartender. Did it stand to reason that Lisa would want to be more like Lori or could it have been the other way around?

Or could the conversation have had nothing at all to do with Honey's problem?

Liz decided to get some rest before she had to get up on her platform. She also wanted to give her mind time to relax, because the back and forth of it was starting to give her a hell of a headache.

After Liz left his office Ed Logan put out a call for Mark Tanner. When his right-hand man showed up he told him to send some telegrams.

"About what?"

"I want to know who that woman is."

"Which woman?"

"The one on the platform, you idiot!" Logan snapped. "Check with some of our contacts and see if you can't find out who and what she is. She's obviously not just any woman."

"What do you think she is?" Tanner asked curiously.

"She obviously handles a gun well, and she won't be bought off or scared off."

"You're saying she's a pro?"

"I'm saying that if she is we'd better find out about it," Logan said, "and then get one of our own."

"Do you really think we need to bring a gunman, Mr. Logan?" Tanner asked. "They're . . . unpredictable."

"Are you prepared to go up against a pro, Tanner?" Logan asked.

"Not alone, no," Tanner said, "but nobody says I have to. We can put together enough men to take care of any professional gunman."

"Or woman?"

Tanner shook his head then and said, "I ain't never heard of a gun*woman*."

"Well, you may have now."

"When's the next shipment of whiskey coming in for Honey O'Day?" Logan asked.

"Friday."

"All right, make sure it's taken care of . . . and send those telegrams."

"Right, Boss."

"Actually, Tanner *had* heard stories about women gunfighters, but he'd never believed them, marking them down as just that, stories.

There wasn't a woman alive could outdraw a man with a gun.

CHAPTER NINETEEN

Unaware that Ed Logan was having his men keep a low profile while he checked her out, Liz was surprised that there was no trouble that night. Logan had certainly been angry enough to send a load of his men to bust up Honey's Place. Perhaps he controlled his anger better than most men, who were often like spiteful children when they got mad.

She was taking a break, spelled by Willie up on the platform, when Mike Early walked in with another man. It was the same man he'd been with the first night Liz had seen him in the place.

"Looks like Mike Early has company tonight," she said to Honey. They were sitting at Honey's table together, and the older woman — who had given up the chair against the wall upon request — turned in her chair to take a look.

"I've seen them together before," she said.

"Maybe that's the help he was talking about."

"We'll find out in a minute," Liz said. "They're on their way over here." Liz leaned forward and quickly added, "I have an idea I want to talk to you about, but I'll save it until after they've gone."

Before Honey could comment the two men had reached their table.

"Honey," Early said, "Liz, . . . this is my friend, Alex Pennell."

"I'm very happy to meet two such lovely ladies," Pennell said, smiling widely.

"Hello, Mr. Pennell," Honey said. Liz simply nodded at the man, waiting to hear what else Mike Early had to say.

Pennell was a tall man, slender to the point of skinniness. The Colt on his hip looked well-used and Liz had the feeling that this was the kind of man who wouldn't find much that he wouldn't do for money.

"Alex is the man I told you about, Honey," Early said then, "the one I said might be able to help us out."

"I can't pay you much, Mr. Pennell."

"Mike explained that, ma'am —" Pennell started to say, but Early cut him off quickly.

"Alex and I have made our own deal, Honey," he said, "independant of the one you and I made. Alex will actually be working for me."

"Although I wouldn't mind making myself available to either one of you ladies," Pennell said, quickly, "if the need should ever arise."

"We'll certainly keep that in mind, Mr. Pennell," Honey said, smoothly.

"Alex, please," Pennell said. "Call me Alex."

"Alex," Honey said. "Mike, Liz and I were just discussing something . . ."

"Then I won't hold you up any longer," Early said. "Just let us know what you decide you might need us for, Honey."

"We're at your disposal," Pennell added eagerly, and Liz had the feeling that he and Early were not talking about the same thing at all.

After the two men had walked back to the bar Honey turned to Liz and said, "What's this about an idea, and why didn't you want Mike to hear?"

"I don't quite trust him, Honey," Liz said, "but if we're going to argue that, let's do it another time. For now let me tell you what I have in mind."

"All right, go ahead."

"It's simple, really," Liz said. "You have a replacement shipment of whiskey coming in at the end of the week, don't you? Friday?"

"That's right."

Today was Tuesday.

"All right, I want to go out and meet it and bring it in."

"Alone?"

"No, not alone."

"Mike?"

Liz shook her head.

"I'll take his friend, Alex. You find something for Mike to do here. You know, a distraction."

Liz didn't think that Honey O'Day would have any problem with that.

"What do you hope to accomplish — I mean,

aside from making sure the whiskey gets here in one piece?''

Liz shrugged.

"At least that, but maybe we'll get lucky. Maybe they'll try to hit it again and we can grab one of them. If we can prove that they work for Logan and were acting on his orders, we might be able to force the sheriff into taking action.''

"I doubt that.''

"Well then, we can send for a marshal. The point is, if we can prove that Logan is breaking the law, it would get him off your back and probably ruin him as well.''

"Well,'' Honey said, ''now you've said something I can deal with. You take Pennell and I'll keep Mike busy, but I'm not quite sure I agree with you about not trusting him. After all, there's a piece of this place in it for him, which gives him a personal stake.''

"Maybe,'' Liz said. ''I'm willing to be convinced, Honey. I really am.'' She stood up, hoping to escape any further discussion of the merits of one Mike Early, and said, ''I have to get back on the platform. We'll talk again later.''

"Or tomorrow,'' Honey said. She had turned in her seat to follow Liz's progress, and take a glance across the room toward the man in question.

Liz caught the glance and followed it to Mike Early, then looked at Honey and said, ''Sure, tomorrow.''

Honey O'Day obviously had plans for the night — probably looking into one aspect of the considerable merits of one Mike Early, merits that Liz Archer was already familiar with.

Back up on the platform Liz considered that the

situation had the possibility of becoming very messy. Honey seemed to have been smitten by Early, and whether it was for physical or emotional reasons didn't matter much. Liz was not the jealous type herself — unless it was concerning Tate Gilmore — but it remained to be seen if the same was true of Honey.

And then there was Mike Early, who seemed to have changed overnight. He had to be aware of Honey's feelings, and he seemed intent on using them to his advantage. Liz wouldn't have thought him capable of that, but she had been wrong about men before. Mike Early may very well have been a decent man who was suddenly confronted with an opportunity he just couldn't pass up.

Liz was just hoping to keep anybody from getting hurt — emotionally or physically.

CHAPTER TWENTY

To the further surprise of everyone concerned at Honey's Place, the remainder of the week passed uneventfully. Liz knew that the one incident at the saloon hardly comprised Ed Logan's entire plan. What was the man up to?

When Friday came around, Liz caught up with Alex Pennell while Early was in Honey's office, doing whatever the two of them did when that door closed behind them.

"Alex."

Pennell turned from the bar, where he was enjoying a cup of coffee. Breakfast was past, and the two men had not been accepted into the "inner circle" yet to the point where they would be included.

"Hello, Liz," Pennell said, smiling. When he smiled his face changed and Liz could see that he did possess some natural charm if he would just stop trying to overdo it with words. "I can call you Liz, can't I?"

"Of course."

"We haven't had much chance to talk and get acquainted."

"That's true," Liz said, "but we could fix that right now, if you like . . . Alex."

"What did you have in mind?"

"How about a little ride?"

That sentence meant one thing when spoken within the confines of Sadie's House, but Pennell was smart enough to know it didn't mean the same thing here.

Still, it sounded like a good start.

"Sure," he said, "let's take a ride."

He started for Honey's office and Liz said, "Where are you going?"

"To let Mike know . . ."

"Mike and Honey are . . . busy, Alex. Besides, do you need Mike Early's permission to go for a ride with me?"

He was still leaning in the direction of Honey's office, and now he leaned back again. As she'd hoped — and expected — he responded to the challenge in her tone.

"No, I guess not. Let's go."

They walked to the livery where they each saddled their own horse, and then rode out of town side by side.

A few miles out of town Alex called out, "Hey, wait a minute."

"What's wrong?" she asked. "Is Blossom going too fast for your horse?"

"That's not the point," he said, "Where are we headed? I thought we were just going to take a ride to get better acquainted."

"We are taking a ride."

"Yeah, but you haven't said a word to me since we left town."

"I'm sorry, Alex," she said, touching his arm. "I guess I just need some help learning how to relax."

Pennell's face brightened and he said, "I can teach you that, Liz."

"A little farther, Alex," she said, squeezing his forearm reassuringly. "There's something farther on that I want to share with you."

"Well, all right," he said, smiling broadly. "Lead the way."

They rode a few more miles and suddenly Liz reined in.

"Is this it?" he asked, looking around. All he could see were rocks and sagebrush and about fifty yards off a wagon approaching.

"What's that?" he asked.

"That's Honey's whiskey delivery."

He looked at her very deliberately and said, "That's what you wanted to show me?"

"I'm sorry, Alex," Liz said, innocently. "What did you have in mind?"

Pennell looked angry, but controlled it saying, "Later, I'll show you later. Would you mind telling me what we are here for?"

"Not at all. We're here to make sure that *this* shipment gets through safely."

"I see, and are we expecting someone to try and make sure it doesn't?"

"We have an open mind about that."

"You know," Pennell said, and now his look was an admiring one, "you're really something."

"Thank you, Alex," she said, and then frowned and added, "I think."

Honey O'Day was worried.

She and Mike Early were in her room, in her bed, but she was worried. She was supposed to be distracting him, but she was the one who was distracted. After seeing Early around town so often she knew that she was attracted to him, but after the first time he'd taken her, right there on the desk in her office, she knew that she was in love with him.

Now she was deceiving him, and she was uncomfortable about it, yet she couldn't tell him because what Liz Archer was doing she wasn't doing for herself, but for Honey's Place.

Liz Archer was the other thing she was worried about. Honey knew that she was older than both Liz and Early, and she knew that they'd probably been together at least once. If Liz wanted him, would she be able to take him?

"What's wrong?" Early asked.

Honey was lying on top of him with her big breasts flattened against his chest. His hands were clutching her buttocks and his mouth had been avidly devouring her nipples when he sensed that something was wrong.

"Nothing."

"Something's on your mind."

"You are."

"I'm right here."

"For how long?"

"What's that mean?"

"Nothing . . ."

"Don't say that again," he said, his strong hands squeezing her cheeks until they hurt.

"I'm older than you, Mike."

"So what?"

"How long before you have what you want, a piece of my place, and forget about me. Or before you want a younger woman, like one of my girls, or . . ."

"Or who?"

"Or Liz Archer. I know you and she were together at least once."

"Did she tell you that?"

"She didn't have to."

"So what if we were?" he asked, kneading her ass now instead of squeezing it. "I'm here now, aren't I?"

"Yes, you are, Mike," she said, "and I want you to stay here."

She decided that she'd use the only means she knew of to try to keep him. It had been some years since Honey O'Day was really a whore named Honey Odell, but she remembered all of her old skills, and she intended to use them now.

She slid down, enjoying the way his body hairs chafed her big nipples, and when she was nestled with her face between his legs she grasped his large erection and began licking it. When she took it in her mouth she was gratified to hear him moan aloud and feel him raise his hips off the bed. She had him now, and if she wanted to keep him she had to make sure he knew that she could give him something no other woman could.

Liz and Pennell rode to meet the wagon and Liz identified herself to the driver.

"Don't make much difference to me who you are, missy," the man said, "long as Honey O'Day is waiting at the other end."

The driver was a portly man in his mid-fifties, somewhat grizzled and used up looking.

As they rode alongside of him, one on either side, Liz asked, "Are you the driver who lost the other load?"

"I didn't lose it!" he said, defensively. "In fact, it wasn't even took from me, it was just . . . destroyed. It's a sin, what they did to perfectly good whiskey."

"I can't argue with that," Alex Pennell said.

Liz looked across the driver at Pennell, who seemed to have retained his good humor, and she wondered idly if he could have been one of the men who'd shot up the first load.

"I'll tell you something else, too," the driver said. "If it happens again they can get somebody else to drive this route. If I want to risk my life I'll go back to driving army supply wagons, or stagecoaches."

"Where was it they stopped you?"

"About two miles farther ahead, a good two miles outside of town."

"Well then, we'd better keep our eyes open."

"I decided that a little while ago after you tricked me into coming out here," Pennell said. "I'm gonna have to keep my eyes open around you, Liz."

"Just keep them open, Alex," she said. "*That's* what I brought you out here for."

"Sorry to hear *that*," he said, half to himself. "I had something different in mind."

"I'm sure you did."

"You two married?" the driver asked.

"Hell no," Liz said.

"You sure act it," the driver said, and urged his team on faster.

Liz and Pennell exchanged a look but neither spoke as they spurred their horses on to catch up.

CHAPTER TWENTY-ONE

Inside of a mile Pennell suddenly held up his hand and said, "Hold it."

Liz looked over at him warily, and the driver of the rig reined in his team.

"What's wrong?"

Pennell lifted his head as if he were sniffing the air, then looked around.

"There," he said, pointing into the distance in an easterly direction.

Liz squinted, and then saw it.

"Dust."

"Must be more than a rider or two to kick up that much dust," Pennell said.

Was he guessing, or did he actually know?

"What do we do?" the driver asked.

Pennell looked at Liz and she said, "Go ahead."

"If we continue on this road they'll intercept us,"

Pennell said to both of them. "We can head west a ways, then cut back in ahead to town. We might avoid them that way."

The driver, as if sensing that Liz was actually in charge, looked at her and said, "That what you want to do, missy?"

"It sounds like as good an idea as any."

"Let's get to it, then," he said, and headed his team west. "You'd better take the lead, son," he said to Pennell, " 'cause I ain't got any idea where we're headed, now."

"Follow me," Pennell said, and Liz couldn't help wondering if he was taking them to safety, or into a trap.

Honey laid in bed and watched Mike Early get dressed. From all appearances he was a little weak in the legs, and she felt good about that. She'd drained him, gotten him all filled up, and drained him again. She was convinced that no woman had ever done for him what she'd just done, but did that give her a big enough hold on him?

"Speaking of your friend Liz, where is she?" he asked, strapping on his gun.

She frowned and said, "I don't know. Why?"

He looked at her and smiled, saying, "Don't worry. I'm also wondering where Alex is."

"Maybe they're together?"

"Liz and Alex?"

"Would that bother you?"

She saw him frown for a moment, but then it was gone and he said, "No, why should it?"

"I don't know."

"I've got to find Alex, Honey," he said. "I'll see you a little later."

"All right."

She didn't try to stop him from going because Liz and Pennell should have met the wagon by now. She laid back on the bed and tried to examine her feelings. It took her only a few moments to realize how frightened she was. She'd never been in love before, so how did she know this was it? Maybe she just *wanted* Mike Early because he was young and handsome.

Now she was worried and afraid, and, for a woman who had been in control of her feelings ever since she'd fucked her first man at thirteen because she knew it would get her a piece of candy, that was frightening.

They continued west with Pennell in the lead, the wagon next, and Liz bringing up the rear.

"I think we've lost them," she called out after an hour.

Pennell stopped and turned in his saddle, peering past Liz. She found herself studying every move he made, to see if it was practiced.

"We'd better keep going west a little longer, don't you think, pop?"

"Don't call me pop," the older man said, "and no, I don't think. I think I want to do whatever this lady wants to do." He leaned over to look back at Liz and asked, "How about it, missy? What do you want to do?"

"I want to head for town."

Pennell looked at both of them and said, "Fine, let's head to town."

They started heading for Loganville again, riding three abreast, but this time the wagon wasn't between them.

"Why do I get the feeling you don't trust me?"

"Don't take it personal," she said. "There aren't very many people I do trust."

"Name one."

Tate Gilmore's name came to mind, but she didn't mention it.

"I can't think of one, right now."

"What about Mike Early?"

"What about him?"

"Do you trust him?"

"About as much as I trust you."

Pennell smiled, as if he was glad to hear that.

"Well, at least that puts me even with him. That is, unless . . ."

"Unless what?"

"Unless you've already slept with him?"

"Did he tell you that?"

"No, he didn't." When an answer was not forthcoming he said, "Did you?"

"And do you think you have a chance to get me to sleep with you?" she asked, ignoring his question.

"Well, I think I've got a better than even chance, yeah." Again there was no reply so he said, "Why not? You could do a lot worse."

"Tell me something, Alex."

"Anything."

"Why'd you go to work for Logan?"

"That's easy. For the money."

"Then why are you working for Honey, now?"

"I'm not," Pennell said, "I'm working for Mike Early."

"Can he pay you more than Logan was?"

She was watching his face and thought she detected some discomfort with the present line of conversation.

"There are . . . other considerations," Pennell said.

"Like what?"

"Like you," Pennell said, "or like one of the other girls who work in that place."

"You like women, huh?"

"I love women, and there's nothing wrong with that," he said, defensively. "Of course, I don't think I've ever run across a woman like you, before."

She ignored the compliment.

"And to you a woman would be enough compensation for the money you're losing by quitting Logan?"

"Well . . ."

"Or are you still working for Ed Logan? You and Mike Early?"

"Missy," the driver called back, interrupting any reply he might have given.

She looked up and saw why the driver had called her. Ahead, coming towards them, were four men on horseback, riding abreast of each other. They weren't riding particularly fast, but then they were doing considerably more than just trotting along. She gave Pennell a look, but he only shrugged and assumed an innocent look.

"Whatever happens," he said gently, like a teacher giving a lesson, "remember, I'm the one who wanted to keep heading west."

She couldn't argue that, but that didn't necessarily clear him.

"Pull up," she told the driver.

"Why?"

"You want to make a run for it with your wagon?" she asked. "You'll end up doing their job for them."

He pulled up and said, "What are we gonna do, then?"

"We're going to wait for them and see what they want." She turned to look at Pennell and said, "Now's your chance, Alex."

"To do what?"

"To make me trust you."

He smiled and said, "All I ever wanted was a chance with you."

"Do me a favor, Alex."

"What?"

"Stay where I can see you."

They waited patiently while the approaching men came closer and closer. The only sign of impatience was on the driver, who didn't quite know what to do with his hand.

Liz saw him start to reach beneath his seat and asked, "What have you got there?"

"Scattergun."

"Leave it there. If you take it out you might spook them."

"If I leave it I might end up dead, this time."

"You won't."

He looked at Pennell, who shrugged, and the driver obeyed, leaving the shotgun where it was.

As the men came into clear view Liz asked Pennell, "You know who they are?"

"Why would I?"

"Don't kid me, Alex," she said. "They're Ed Logan's men, and you either were, or you still are."

"Liz —"

"Do they know what you're up to? Or are they going to think that because you're here with me you've gone and changed sides?"

"All right," Pennell said, "they're Logan's men, but they're only after the whiskey, Liz. Let them have it."

"No."

"You can't face them alone."

"I'm not alone, I've got you, and the driver."

"The driver? What good's he gonna' do you?"

"And what about you, Alex?" she asked. "What good are you going to do me?"

"Liz, I —"

"Here they come, Alex," she said as the men approached. "I guess we're about to find out the answer to that question."

CHAPTER TWENTY-TWO

Pennell was next to Liz and a little forward of her, so that she could see him as well as the others. She hoped that if the need did arise for the driver to produce his shotgun, he'd make the most of it. It was bad enough if she and Pennell were facing four men, but if Pennell sided with them she'd be facing five.

As the riders reined their horses in about twenty feet away from them, Liz reached up, pulled her orange bandana out from beneath her collar and unfurled it. Pennell saw her do this and his eyes widened.

He said nothing, but made a quick decision.

"Where are you folks headed?" one of the men asked.

"To Loganville," Liz replied.

"With that whiskey?"

"That's right."

The man exchanged glances with his three colleagues, then looked at Liz and said, "I'm afraid not. You can go on ahead, but the wagon stays here."

"I don't have time to argue the point with you," Liz said. "Please move aside."

The man looked at Pennell and asked, "Who you siding with here, Pennell?"

"I'm over here, ain't I, Stillwell?" Pennell said, and Liz thought that he didn't sound too happy about it.

"You're making a bad mistake, Pennell. Nobody goes against Ed Logan."

"You're the ones making a mistake, Stillwell, Parks, you others," Pennell said. "You don't know what you're dealing with here."

"What are you talking about?" Parks asked.

"Take a good look at this lady here."

"What about her?"

"Take the time to study her," Pennell said. "What do you see?"

"I see a lot of woman going to waste if she don't ride for town right now," Stillwell said.

"All right," Pennell said, resignedly. "I want you boys to remember that I tried to warn you."

"About what?" Stillwell asked.

"About dying."

The four men exchanged glances again, but none of them made a move to leave.

"We're not going anywhere, Pennell. Maybe you'd better start riding. We don't have any orders about you, only this whiskey and this woman."

"Well," Pennell said, "since I'm already sitting at the table I guess I'll stay and take a hand."

"Your choice," Stillwell said. He turned his attention to Liz and said, "One last chance, miss. Ride off and leave this here wagon."

"I can't do that."

"What about you, driver?"

The driver ran his hand across his mouth and visions of the past, when he was driving a supply wagon for the army, and back even further when he was a scout, sprang into his head.

"Well," he said, "I reckon I'll just stay put, son. You go ahead and do what you got to do."

Liz immediately felt better about the man, and about their chance of keeping the whiskey intact.

"It's your move, Stillwell," she said.

"Crazy," the man said, and went for his gun.

The three men with him had been waiting for his move, and when he made it they reached for their guns as well.

None of the four men were particularly fast with their guns, and Liz saw this right away. She also saw that the driver had produced his shotgun quick enough.

She drew her Colt and fired at Stillwell, her first shot taking him from the saddle with a look of surprise on his face. She heard Pennell's gun fire and Parks fell. On the heels of that, the driver's shotgun barked and he almost cut one of the other men clean in half. Liz fired a second time, and the fourth man slumped over his saddle and then slid to the ground very slowly, inch by inch, and they watched until he finally hit the ground with a dull thud.

"Well," Pennell said, holstering his gun. "That wasn't too bad."

"Whooee!" the driver exploded, "don't that get the blood boiling again after all these years."

"You're pretty handy with that shotgun," Liz said to him. "Why didn't you use it last time?"

"To tell you the truth, miss, I was just plain scared, but seeing you stand up to these yahoos put me all to shame. I'm glad you came along, 'cause you just about made me into a man, again."

"And a hell of a man, too, friend," Liz said. "What's your name?"

"Carter, miss, my name is Jasper Carter."

"Well, Jasper, how did the whiskey come through?"

"Just fine. Those four never even got off a shot."

"Good. Don't you think it's time we got it delivered, then?"

"I surely do, Miss," he said, stowing his shotgun beneath his seat and picking up his reins, "I surely do."

As they started to ride towards town again Pennell watched while Liz curled her bandana up again and tucked it down inside her collar.

"Ain't no point in hiding it now, Liz," he said. "I've seen it, already."

"So?"

"I heard stories, but thought they were just stories."

"About what?"

"About you . . . Angel Eyes."

"Well, I don't suppose it hurts that you know, Alex. That is, unless you plan to tell Logan."

"I could you know," he said. "Nobody but that

driver saw what happened here today, and he'll leave just as soon as he makes his delivery. Logan doesn't have to know that I helped you kill four of his men. He might pay handsomely for the information that he's dealing with Angel Eyes."

"If you were going to do that, Alex," she said, "I don't think you would have sided with me. Speaking of that, why did you side with me?"

"What do you mean? I'm working for Mike, ain't I? This is his whiskey, isn't it?"

"Not for a while, it isn't," Liz said. "He doesn't get a piece of Honey's Place until Logan is taken care of."

"Well, we've just taken care of four of his men, that's a good start, isn't it?"

"I guess it is," Liz said, eyeing the man cautiously. True, he had killed one of Logan's men, but that still didn't mean she trusted him completely.

"What do you know about that," he said, half to himself, "I'm working with Angel Eyes."

The knowledge of that made him all the more anxious to get her into bed.

"What do you want?" Ed Logan asked Mark Tanner in an annoyed tone. The mess of paperwork on his desk made it clear what had put him in such a bad mood. Tanner was glad he was just a worker, and not involved with the business aspect of Logan's operation.

"I got a reply on one of those telegrams I sent out," he said, showing the piece of paper to Logan.

"Already? What about the others?"

"They'll probably take longer, but this one from San Francisco came back in a few hours."

"Well, what's it say?"

"According to your man in San Francisco this woman was there a few months ago and raised some hell."

"Well then, what's her game, damn it? Who the hell is she?"

"If it's the same woman," Tanner said, "her name is Liz Archer —"

"I know that!"

"— and they call her 'Angel Eyes.' "

Logan stared and then said, "That's just a story."

"I'm afraid it's not, Boss," Tanner said. "I didn't believe it, either, so I sent a second telegram to confirm it." He showed the man the second piece of paper and said, "It's confirmed. 'Angel Eyes' really does exist."

"Well," Logan said, "even if there is such a person, that doesn't mean that this is the same woman."

"But if she is —"

"If she is," Ed Logan said, "she's still just a damned female."

"Boss —"

"Get out, Tanner, and see if you can't hurry the replies on those other telegrams. I need time to think."

"Okay, Boss."

Mark Tanner left Ed Logan's office and stopped out in the hall to reread the two telegrams. Logan's San Francisco source had always been reliable, so there was no reason to think that this time he wasn't. That meant that there really was a female gunfighter called "Angel Eyes," and this was a blow to a man like Mark Tanner.

How could a woman ever outdraw a man, and kill him? It was inconceivable to him, and he was actually looking forward to seeing this woman in action.

Hopefully, she'd lose, but at least he'd get to see her.

After Tanner had left Logan sat back and stared at the ceiling. He'd heard the stories about a woman with golden hair and the eyes of an angel, who could outdraw any man, and he'd marked them down as flights of fancy, dime-novel stories created by some over imaginative writer.

But if it was true, if there really was such a person and she was in Loganville, it could mean a lot of publicity. People with those kinds of reputations — Hickok, Wes Hardin, Clint Adams and the like — were fair prey for anyone who could put them under, and to be the man who did it — or engineered it — would bring Ed Logan the notice that he needed to further his political career.

He needed someone, though, someone who would take care of her for money and not worry about who got the credit. That meant he needed a real pro, and he thought he knew just who that person could be.

CHAPTER TWENTY-THREE

Mike Early was on Loganville's main street when he saw Liz Archer, Alex Pennell and Jasper Carter coming with the whiskey wagon. It was late afternoon and Early had been looking for Pennell for most of the day.

When they pulled up in front of Honey's Place Early put his hands on his hips and said to Pennell, "Where the hell have you been?"

"I was lured out of town on false pretenses," Pennell said with an amused look on his face.

Early was less than amused however, especially when he noticed the exchange of glances between Liz and Pennell.

"You've got some explaining to do, Alex."

"Don't push me, Mike," Pennell said, his face losing his good humor. "Not out here on the street. You want to talk we'll talk in private."

Early and Pennell exchanged hard glances then and at that moment Liz realized that the two men were not really good friends.

"Well," Liz said, "while you boys have your little talk Jasper and Willie will get the whiskey unloaded. Of course, it would go much faster if you two helped."

"I'll help," Pennell said, dismounting.

"So will I," Early said. "We can talk later."

"Fine," Pennell said.

"I'll take the horses to the livery, Alex."

Pennell handed Liz the reins and as she was leaving she heard Early yelling for Willie to come out.

More and more she saw something new in Mike Early, and she liked none of it. Pennell, on the other hand, was becoming increasingly interesting to her.

Ed Logan looked out his window at the exact moment Mike Early carried in the last load of whiskey from the wagon.

"What the hell!" Logan snapped.

He grabbed his hat and stormed out of his office. Somebody had a lot of explaining to do.

When the whiskey was all carried into the saloon Honey looked at Liz and said, "Well, it looks like your idea worked. Did you have any trouble?"

"Some," Liz said, "but Alex, Jasper and I were able to handle it. I'm afraid Ed Logan is going to be a few men short from now on."

"He'll rehire," Pennell said. "There's no shortage

of men willing to work for the wages Logan pays. They just have to be able to take orders.''

"What about you?" Liz asked as Honey walked over to supervise the handling of the whiskey now that it was inside the saloon.

"Me? I've never been very good at taking orders — which is something your friend Mike Early might find out pretty quick.''

"I thought you were working *for* Mike," Liz said. "Doesn't that mean you have to take his orders?''

"Our relationship is a little more different than that," Pennell said. "Actually, we're more like partners.''

"Does he know that?''

"Not yet," Pennell said, grinning, "but he'll find out. How would you like to have dinner with me?''

The question came very quickly, and Liz didn't even have time to be surprised at her response.

"I would like that very much."

Honey was behind the bar with Lori, the bartender twin, when Mike Early came over and said to Lori, "Get lost for a while.''

Lori looked at Honey, who nodded, and only then did the girl leave.

"Look, Mike," Honey said, "I don't mind you feeling your oats, but don't start ordering my girls around.''

"What about after we become partners?''

"We'll have to discuss in detail just what kind of partnership that will be.''

"We can do that later," Early said. "Right now I

want to know why I wasn't informed about this whiskey shipment, and about Liz and Alex going out to meet it.''

"For the same reason you can't order my girls around,'' Honey said. "You don't have a piece of this place yet.''

Early touched her arm and said, "I thought we were . . . partners.''

"We are,'' Honey said in a low voice, "in bed, not in business. I've worked hard for a long time to get a place of my own, Mike, and I'm not going to just give away a part of it . . . to anyone.''

"All right,'' Early said, backing off, "all right. I can understand that.''

"Thank you.''

"I think after you've got all of this liquor squared away we should all get together to talk about our next move.''

"That's fine with me,'' Honey said, "I'll tell Liz.''

"And I'll bring Alex.''

"Why Pennell?''

"Why Liz?''

"She's here to help me, Mike.''

"Alex is here to help me.''

"All right, all right,'' she said, giving in. "After closing tonight, we'll all talk.''

"Fine.''

"Can I get back to work now?''

"By all means,'' Early said, "get back to work.''

Liz was outside the saloon when Early came out behind her and grabbed her by the arm.

"Let go, Mike!"

"We have to talk."

"Not right now," she said, pulling her arm free. "I have to take a bath."

"That's perfect," he said. "We'll take one together."

"Forget it."

"Why?"

"In case you can't tell, that lady in there is in love with you."

"That's one of the things we have to talk about."

"Talk to Honey about it," Liz said. "You know, Mike, you're not the same man I slept with the other night."

"Sure I am," he argued. "I'm just a little smarter now, that's all."

"Smart? You call playing both ends against the middle smart?"

"What do you mean?"

"I don't know what I mean," she said, "not exactly. I only know that I don't trust your motives and I'm not going to take my eyes off you. I think you're out to cheat Honey out of her place."

"And what about Logan?"

"That's where it gets dangerous, Mike, because I think you're out to cheat him, too."

"I'm not cheating anyone," he said. "I'm just trying to do what's good for me for a change."

"That's fine, you do what's good for you. I'm going to do what's good for Honey, because I like her and I don't want to see her lose this place — not even a small part of it."

"Liz, let's have dinner and talk . . ."

"I have a dinner engagement already," she said, "and you're making me late in getting ready. Excuse me."

"An engagement with who?" he called out, but she ignored him and kept on walking.

Alex Pennell came out of the saloon behind Mike Early and slapped the bigger man on the back.

"Woman trouble, Mike?" he asked. "Having trouble keeping them all in line? Why don't you go over to Sadie's tonight, work out some of your aggressions."

Mike Early may have changed over the past week or so, but he hadn't changed that much.

"I don't pay for it, Alex. You know that."

"Well, you're missing a lot," Pennell said. "You know, when you pay them they work a little harder for you."

Early thought of the way Honey O'Day had worked over him that morning — his legs were still a little weak — and said, "That's not necessarily true."

"Well, I'll see you later, then."

Early turned and said, "I still want to talk to you, Alex."

"Ease up, Mike," Pennell said. "Everything is fine. We'll talk later."

As Pennell walked away Early again thought of Honey and the time he'd spent with her that morning. She'd seemed to have something on her mind when they first started out, and then later she'd become rather desperate about the sex.

Could it have been that she was trying to keep his mind off something? Or keep him occupied?

Early thought back to the previous week when all he did was work for Ed Logan. He'd had less problems then, but he'd also had less prospects. No, all in all he was better off, now. He just had to make sure that he kept the people around him in line, and since he was much smarter than all of them, that shouldn't be too hard. He was the most educated of all of them — Honey, Logan, Liz — and he was going to put that education to good use.

By the time Ed Logan found Mark Tanner in one of the smaller of Loganville's saloons — owned by Logan of course — he was livid.

"Honey O'Day's whiskey just got delivered," he said, sitting down opposite his man.

"What?"

"It came in with that woman and Pennell. And none of the men are back," Logan added. "Get somebody to go out there and find out what happened."

"I'll tell you what happened," Tanner said. "They ran into a lady called Angel Eyes."

"You buy that story now, huh?"

"I got one more telegram back, Boss, and I'd say it's confirmed. I don't know how good she really is, but apparently she's for real."

"Well," Logan said, "maybe we just better find out how good she is, huh?"

CHAPTER TWENTY-FOUR

Liz and Pennell had dinner in the small cafe where she'd eaten before.

"Tell me something, Alex," she said as they were eating.

"Anything."

"Are you and Mike friends?"

"Are you asking me a question about me," he asked, "or about Mike?"

"About you."

"Then I'll answer it. Mike and I got along up to now because we were both odd men out. By that I mean that neither one of us fit in with Logan's other men, so occasionally we found ourselves having a drink together, or getting something to eat together. Are we friends? I think the answer to that is no."

"He's changed quite a bit over the past week, don't you think?"

"He's changed a lot," Pennell said. "He used to be a quiet, almost shy guy. I never understood why he started to work for Logan. He was always so smart, and then all of a sudden he seems to . . ."

"All of a sudden what?"

"Nothing."

"I'll tell you, then," she said. "He said it to me today. He's out for himself."

"He's a smart man," Pennell said. "Smarter than me, smarter than Logan, I think. If he put his mind to it he could probably do real well for himself."

"Well, I think he's putting his mind to it," Liz said. "I think he's got Logan and Honey thinking that he's working for them and he's really working for himself."

Pennell didn't say anything.

"Alex, what do you want out of this?"

"Just a stake," he said, "so I can be on my way."

"Is that what Mike promised you?"

"Yes."

"You could have gotten that from Logan."

"I don't like Logan."

"And you like Mike?"

"I did."

"When did you start working for Logan?"

"About three weeks ago. Mike was already working for him, if that's your next question."

"It was, and now you've both quit?"

"Well, I haven't exactly put it in writing . . ."

"What's Logan going to do when he sees you and Mike working for Honey?"

"Maybe he'll get mad," Pennell said, "maybe he'll make a mistake."

"Is that what Mike said?"

"Liz, you don't trust me, right?"

"Not all the way."

"Well, I feel the same way about everybody," Pennell said. "Can we drop this conversation?"

"Alex —"

"Let me just say one thing."

"What?"

"I wouldn't do anything, or let Mike do anything, that would hurt you."

"Oh, Alex . . ." she said, shaking her head in exasperation.

Later she told herself that she never thought she'd end up in bed with Alex Pennell.

Still later she admitted that was a lie . . . .

After dinner Alex asked her to go to his room with him.

"Where do you live? In a hotel or boardinghouse?"

"Neither. When I came to town I found a room above the General Store. I don't like hotels, and I like boardinghouses even less. Besides, Logan owns most of them in this town."

"What about the General Store?"

"He owns that, too, but I pay the guy who runs the store for the room."

After a moment of silence he said, "What do you say?"

"Do I owe you this for this afternoon?"

He shook his head and said, "You don't owe me anything Liz."

That was when she decided that she would go with him.

Now as she watched him undress she realized that he was almost as skinny as he appeared to be when dressed, but there was a leather toughness to him. He was not muscular like Mike, but he was not weak, either, not by a longshot.

When he was undressed she stared at him, amazed. He was impressively endowed, and his penis was only semi-erect. Fully erect he'd be larger than Mike Early, larger than a lot of men she'd known.

"I've been with a lot of women, Liz . . ." he said.

She began to undress and said, "That sounds like a confession."

"It is."

"Well, it's out of place, here. You don't owe me any explanations, and I don't owe you any."

Fully nude she approached him and put her hands on his shoulders.

"All we owe each other right now is some pleasure and some relaxation. All right?"

For his answer he reached for her breasts, and she closed her eyes, surprised at how gentle his touch was. She could feel his swollen tip prodding her and reached down to take it in both hands.

When he kissed her she pushed her tongue into his mouth and he slid his hands around her, down her back until they were clutching her buttocks, holding her tightly to him. She slid one hand up his side and could feel the outline of his ribs.

"You could use some extra weight," she said, teasing him.

"It would slow me down . . ."

He lifted her into his arms then, easily, as if to prove that he could, and deposited her onto the bed. He stared down at her, convinced that he'd never seen anything or anyone as beautiful before.

She lifted her arms and said, "Come on, Alex. I want you."

That was the best news he'd heard in a long time.

Mark Tanner was out with a couple of men, trying to find out what happened to the four men they'd sent out to stop the whiskey. Ed Logan took advantage of the man's absence to send a telegram of his own, one which he wanted no one to know about.

After he sent it off he didn't bother to wait for a reply. He knew that the man he was sending for would come. He'd used the man before, sparingly, and it had been some time since he'd last used him, but this situation called for a professional. He was convinced that the only thing standing between him and Honey's Place was Liz Archer.

Alex Pennell's head was buried between Liz Archer's legs and his knowing tongue was working wonders, darting in and out and around until she was ready to scream.

"Alex —" she gasped, and anything else she might have said was cut off by the rush of her orgasm. She lifted her hips off the bed as his tongue probed and circled, his lips sucked, and she turned her head into the pillow so that her scream would not be heard.

It was her turn after that, and she swirled her tongue around the bulbous head of his cock, holding onto the thick, heavily veined stalk with both hands as she started to suck, taking as much of him as she could into her mouth and then letting him slide free so that the breeze cooled her saliva on him and gave him the chills.

As her head moved up and down, her right fist began to move in the opposite direction. Her left hand fondled his heavy balls and as she felt him swelling in her mouth she took some of his pubic hair between her thumb and forefinger and pulled on it. He cried out as he ejaculated, pain and pleasure mingling into one.

And still later he was on top of her, and then inside of her, the entire length of him nestled tightly within her as she wrapped her legs around his slim waist and began bouncing her butt off the bed, meeting his hard thrusts. The tempo increased until they were literally pounding away at each other. As she heard him moan and felt him explode inside of her, she reached a second orgasm and bit down on his bony shoulder to muffle her screams.

Afterward she said, "I think I have bruises."

"Where?"

"All over," she said, stroking him. "You're very bony."

"You're very beautiful."

"Thank you."

"I have a bite on my shoulder."

"I'm sorry," she said, putting her hand to it.

"It's all right."

"It's not bleeding."

"Does that mean that you want to try again?"

She giggled and slid her hand between his legs, saying, "Definitely."

He was semi-hard in her hand seconds later and as she stroked him to complete fullness she said, "Alex?"

"What?"

"I hope you don't think that this means I trust you now."

"You know something?"

"What?"

"You and I have a lot in common."

"What does that mean?"

"We don't trust anyone."

"Which means we just naturally can't trust each other."

"It's a good thing this," he said, putting a hand on one of her breasts, "has nothing to do with trust."

Mark Tanner reported to Ed Logan in his office immediately upon returning to town. His discovery had shaken him, and now it shook his employer.

"They're dead," he said, "they're all dead."

"How?"

"Shot."

"Damn! She's going through my men like they don't exist."

"These are the first ones she's killed."

Tanner didn't bother telling Logan that one of the men had been killed by a shotgun, and the other three by a pistol. Hell, she killed three, she could have killed all four just as easy.

"And they'll be the last ones she kills," Logan swore with feeling. "I've already made arrangements to take care of that."

"What arrangements?"

Logan looked at Tanner and asked, "Have you ever heard of a man named Dack Mulligan?"

"Mulligan?" Tanner said, frowning at the name. "No, I haven't. Why? Who is he?"

"He's a pro, Tanner," Logan said. "A man who makes his living with a gun."

"But I've never heard of him."

"I said he was a pro, didn't I?"

CHAPTER TWENTY-FIVE

The next few days were tense, and for more reasons than just Ed Logan.

Actually, there was no trouble from Ed Logan or any of his men at all, and Liz Archer had to wonder what the man was waiting for. He had to retaliate for what had happened to the men he'd sent to intercept the whiskey delivery, but why hadn't he, yet?

No, the tension came from within their own camp.

Liz and Honey were wary around each other, as were Early and Pennell. There was also a certain amount of tension between Liz and Early, Honey and Early, Liz and Pennell. The only people who seemed to have no problem with each other were Honey and Pennell, because they wanted nothing from each other.

There were others, though. Lori and Lisa, the sisters, seemed to be having some trouble, as well.

Lisa had sufficiently recovered from her attack to come back to work, and both Honey and Liz noticed the tension. Of course, Liz was the only one who knew about the overheard conversation because she hadn't shared it with anyone else. She also hadn't been able to verify whether or not what they were talking about was Lori having something to do with one of Logan's men, and passing information on.

The rest of the girls knew about Logan's intention to take over and sensed that something was going on among the people who were supposed to be preventing it. This made them nervous, as well.

Everybody seemed to be walking on eggshells, waiting for the other boot to drop.

CHAPTER TWENTY-SIX

Dack Mulligan rode into Loganville and was unimpressed by what he saw. He'd last been there almost eight months before and the town hadn't changed a hair.

Mulligan had worked for Logan often in the old days, and when Logan had first taken over the town it had grown in leaps and bounds. Now, after eight months, there were no signs of progress anywhere that he could see, so his guess was that Ed Logan had lost interest. Always an ambitious man, Logan undoubtedly had his sites set higher than running a town in Wyoming.

Mulligan rode his horse to the livery and handed it over to the liveryman. After that he went to the hotel, checked in, dropped his gear in his room, and went to see Ed Logan.

Logan's office was in the same place, so he mounted the stairs and opened the door to his office without knocking.

"Dack!" Logan said.

Something else hadn't changed, Mulligan saw with some satisfaction, and that was the fact that Dack Mulligan was the only man that "Big" Ed Logan feared.

"I'd just about given up on you."

"That's funny," Mulligan said, "because I gave up on you months ago."

"I know you haven't heard from me in quite some time . . ."

"I just figured somebody had finally killed you."

"That's not funny, Dack."

"Wasn't meant to be."

Mulligan, as large as Logan but somehow more imposing, took the chair in front of Logan's desk and said, "How about a drink?"

"Sure, brandy?"

"Whiskey."

"The brandy's really excellent."

That hadn't changed, either. Logan was always trying to push the brandy on Mulligan.

"Whiskey," Mulligan said, his tone dropping several degrees so that Logan seemed to suddenly feel a chill.

"Sure, Dack."

Logan poured Mulligan a glass of whiskey and himself some brandy.

Mulligan drank the whiskey down, then got up to pour himself another without asking.

"This town is in piss poor shape."

"That may be," Logan said, "but I've got plans that go beyond this town."

"I figured as much when I rode in."

Mulligan drank the second whiskey, poured himself a third, and took it back to his seat. He casually lifted his long legs up and placed the heels of his black leather boots on Logan's desk. Logan was glad to see that he'd apparently left his spurs in his room.

"What have you got on your mind after eight months, Logan?"

"The same as always, Dack," Logan said. "I want you to kill someone."

Mulligan nodded and asked, "Who?"

"I don't think I've ever asked you to kill a woman before, Dack," Logan said. "Do you have any prejudice against that?"

"No prejudice," Mulligan said, "just a different price."

"Ah," Logan said, "a higher one, I presume."

"Definitely."

"Why?"

Mulligan fixed Logan with a hard, long stare and then said very deliberately, "It's distasteful. Women are not for killing."

"This one is," Logan said. "She's in my way."

"Why do you need me?" Mulligan asked. "You've got a lot of men working for you."

"She's killed four of them already, and made fools of two others."

"That's what a woman. is supposed to do,"

Mulligan said, "make fools of men. How did she kill them?"

"She shot them," Logan said. "She outdrew them."

"One at a time?"

"All at the same time."

A look of interest suddenly crossed Dack Mulligan's face. He dropped his feet from the desk and sat up straight in his chair.

"You know, don't you?" Logan asked. "You know who she is."

"Angel Eyes," Mulligan said, and Ed Logan nodded.

Now he knew she was for real and not just a figment of someone's over active imagination — but then, neither was Dack Mulligan.

It was coincidence that Alex Pennell was on the street when Dack Mulligan rode into town, because Pennell was probably the only person in Loganville, Wyoming, who had ever seen the man before. He knew who Mulligan was, and he knew what his presence meant.

As Mulligan rode into the livery, Pennell went looking for Liz Archer.

Liz was in the saloon, standing underneath her platform, peering up at the bottom.

"What's wrong?" Lori asked, coming up next to her.

"I'm not sure," Liz said, "but I thought I felt it

give a bit when I came down last night."

"Better have somebody check it," Lori suggested.

"I think you're right."

At that moment Alex Pennell came in and both Liz and Lori looked his way.

"I've got to take care of the bar," Lori said, and left as Pennell approached.

"We've got to talk," he said to her, and she had never seen him so serious.

"Don't tell me, let me guess," she said. "One night in bed has convinced you to turn over a new leaf, and you'll never see another woman."

"Not quite," he said. "We've got some company in town today."

"Who?"

"Dack Mulligan."

The only reason Liz Archer knew the name was because when Tate Gilmore had taught her how to handle a gun, he had also briefed her on the men who lived by them. He'd told her about Hickok, Bat Masterson and Wes Hardin, about Clint Adams, Clay Allison and Wyatt Earp, and he'd told her about Dack Mulligan and men like him.

"Mulligan's different," Gilmore had told her, "and there are only a few like him. He hires out his gun and looks for no credit. Consequently, the newspapermen and dime novel writers know nothing about him."

Just like they knew nothing about Tate Gilmore and Liz Archer.

"You know who he is?" Pennell asked.

"Yes, I do," she said, "but how do you know?"

"I saw him in action once, in Abilene. Liz, you know why he's here, don't you?"

"I can guess."

"Somebody's got to be paying him to be here and nobody in this town can afford him except Ed Logan. He's here for you, Liz, for a crack at 'Angel Eyes.' "

"I guess so."

"You've got to get out of town."

"And leave Honey to fend for herself?"

"She won't be. I'll be here."

"And Mike Early?"

"Talk about fending for yourself," Pennell said, wryly.

"Then he is out to get Honey's Place, isn't he?"

"Look, I'll tell you all about it if you promise to leave town right afterward."

"I will not."

"Don't be stubborn!" he snapped. "All that can get you is dead."

"Thanks for the vote of confidence."

"Look, Liz, you may be good, but you're not good enough to face a Dack Mulligan."

"Alex, stop worrying."

"Sure, I'll stop worrying." He grabbed her by the arms and said, "You little idiot —"

"What's going on?"

They both turned in the direction of the voice and saw Mike Early standing just inside the batwing doors.

"Mike, talk some sense into this girl."

"What's wrong?"

"Alex is a worrier," Liz said.

"Dack Mulligan's in town." Pennell said.

"Who's Dack Mulligan?"

"Look," Liz said, "you explain it to him. I've got to find a carpenter."

"Liz —"

"Will somebody tell me what's going on?" Early asked, showing his annoyance.

"Talk to Alex, Mike," Liz said, and left in search of someone to shore up her platform before it gave way beneath her and did Dack Mulligan's job for him.

CHAPTER TWENTY-SEVEN

Mike Early stormed out of the saloon after Alex Pennell explained the situation to him and marched across the street to Ed Logan's office. Pennell went to find Liz to argue with her again.

Early threw the door to Logan's office open and the two men — Logan and Mulligan — turned to look at him.

"What are you trying to pull?" Early demanded.

"What are you doing here, Early?"

Early approached Logan's desk ignoring Mulligan, who remained seated.

"We had a deal."

"And you haven't produced, Early," Logan told him. "You've been having yourself a good old time across the street with all those women, but you haven't done me one bit of good. That Archer bitch killed four of my men!"

"You haven't given me enough time!"

"You've had plenty of time," Logan replied. "I think you're looking out for your own interests here, Early. I think you're taking both Honey O'Day and me for a couple of suckers. As far as I'm concerned, you work for her. You're fired!"

Early flexed his hands open and closed a few times, wanting to grab Logan by the throat. Mulligan saw this and chose that moment to stand up.

"Who is this fella, Logan?" he asked.

"This is an ex-employee of mine, Mulligan," Logan said, "and since you are a present employee of mine, why don't you throw him out of my office?"

"I'm not a bouncer, Logan," Mulligan said, but he was looking at Mike Early when he said it. "I'm a killer. I kill people. You want this man killed?"

Logan looked at Early and said, "What about it, Early? Do I want you killed?"

Continuing to ignore Mulligan, but well aware of his presence, Early pointed a finger at Logan and said, "You haven't heard the last of this, Logan."

As he headed for the door he heard Logan saying, "You'd better find yourself another job, Early. The one you've got now isn't going to last much longer!"

Out on the street Mike Early stopped and caught his breath. If Logan's gunman hadn't been there he probably would have killed him. Still, he wasn't going to get away with what he was doing. Early's salary and bonus from Logan might be gone, but he still had a potential gold mine in Honey's Place.

Earlier on he'd known that he'd make out all right no matter who won. Now it was clear that he needed Honey O'Day to come out on top.

In order for that to happen he needed somebody who could stand up to Dack Mulligan.

He went looking for Alex Pennell.

Dack Mulligan said, "You should have let me kill him."

It was then that Logan realized how much Mulligan loved his work, and he shivered.

"You may have that chance yet Dack, but not in my office."

"Who is he?"

"A turncoat named Mike Early. He talked me into letting him go to work for Honey O'Day —"

"Who's Honey O'Day?"

Logan stopped for a moment, then started again with a different tact.

"Actually, none of this has anything to do with what I want you for. Well, actually, it has, but it's not really something you need to know."

"Why don't you just tell me all about it and let me decide that?"

"All right," Logan said. "There's a saloon across the street that I want . . ."

Pennell, remembering that Liz said she was looking for a carpenter, found her talking to one of the men who had originally installed the platform.

"I'm sure I felt it give, Mr. Simmons, and I'd like you to check it."

"Sure, Miss, I'll check it as soon as I get a chance," the man promised.

"When you get a chance?"

"Liz —" Pennell said, trying to get her attention.

"When will that be?"

"Liz, listen —"

"I don't want to end up on my behind in a bunch of firewood, Mr. Simmons."

"Miss Archer —" Simmons started, but Pennell interrupted him by shouting, "Damn it, Elizabeth!"

"Alex!" she said in exasperation. "Can we talk about this later?"

"We're gonna talk about it right now," he said. He took her arm in a solid grip and she was reminded once again that Pennell was much stronger than he looked.

"I hope you'll take care of that soon, Mr. Simmons . . ." she shouted as Pennell dragged her from the carpenter's store.

Mike Early saw Alex Pennell pulling Liz Archer across the street by the arm and intercepted them.

"We have to talk," he said.

"That's what *we* intend to do," Pennell said, looking meaningfully at Liz.

"No," Early said, "I mean all of us. Honey, too. Let's go over to the saloon."

"All right," Pennell said.

"You can let go, now," Liz said, sweetly.

On the way to the saloon Early said to Pennell, "You told me that Logan brought the gunman in, Alex, but you didn't say who he was here for."

"No," Pennell said, "I didn't, did I?"

Early dropped the matter, intending to pick it up again when they were all together.

CHAPTER TWENTY-EIGHT

They were all gathered in Honey's office: Honey, Early, Pennell, and Liz.

"Are you sure my girls shouldn't be in on this?" Honey asked.

"They'd have nothing to add to this," Early said.

Thinking of Lori and Lisa, Liz wasn't as sure about that as Early was.

"All right, then," Honey said, "what's this all about?"

"Logan has brought in a gunman."

"How do you know?"

"Alex saw him ride into town. His name is Dack Mulligan."

"I never heard of him."

"Explain that to her, Alex."

Pennell shrugged and explained how Mulligan was a pro who didn't want everyone to know his name.

He worked for money and didn't take any credit for his kills. Liz listened and wondered — as she had when Tate Gilmore had first told her about men like Mulligan — how the man managed to maintain such a low profile.

"Why would Logan bring a gunman in? Is he just going to kill us?"

"What we have to worry about first," Early said, "is getting someone to stand up to the man." Early turned to Pennell and said, "Alex, you're pretty good with a gun."

"That may be," Pennell said, "but I'm not in Dack Mulligan's class."

"Who is?"

"Hickok would be, if he were alive. Masterson and Earp might."

"We can't get those people. Who else?"

"Tate Gilmore, probably," Pennell said with a shrug. "I can't think of anyone else," he added with a sidelong look at Liz.

"Go ahead, Alex," Liz said, "lay it all out for them."

"Lay what out?" Honey asked.

"What's she talking about?" Early asked.

"She's talking about getting herself killed."

"You want to face Mulligan?" Early asked. "Liz, I know you can handle a gun well for a woman —"

"Well?" Pennell asked. "For a woman? Early open your eyes. Do you know who she is?"

"Know who who is?" Early asked, confusion plain on his face.

"Liz Archer," Alex Pennell said, "is otherwise known as Angel Eyes."

"Angel Eyes," Mike repeated. Looking at Liz he said, "You're Angel Eyes?"

"In the flesh."

"You're sure?" Early asked Pennell.

"I saw her in action, Mike," Pennell reminded him, "but I'm *not* saying she can handle Mulligan. I'm not even sure any of the *men* I mentioned can."

"I thought they were just stories . . ." Early said, staring at Liz. "She's got a rep, Alex."

"A lot of people do. Mulligan doesn't. Think about that. He's been living by his gun a long time Mike, and he's still around. That's because very few people who have seen his move live to tell about it."

"You have," Liz said.

"Yes, you have," Mike said. "What about that Alex?"

Pennell stared at them and said, "All right, here it is. I used to think I was pretty good with a gun. In fact, I am pretty good, but when I crossed some people in Abilene they paid Dack Mulligan to come after me. He outdrew me clean as you please and put a hole in me. He left me for dead, but I didn't die. I'm probably one of the few people who's ever seen him and lived to tell about it. That's why I'm telling you," he added, looking at Liz, "this man is as fast as . . . as magic!"

"All right," Early said, "so that leaves you out. He's already beat you, and he'd do it again."

"I didn't say that!"

Early, Liz and Honey looked at Alex Pennell who explained, "I was a lot younger then."

"Are you saying you could take him now?" Early asked.

Looking at Liz, Pennell said, "I think I'd have a better chance than Liz."

"You're full of shit, Alex," Liz said, and now all eyes moved to her. "I killed two of those men, remember that."

"They weren't gunmen, Liz."

"You're telling me that you're faster than I am?"

"Come on, Liz," Pennell said, as if the question was just downright silly.

Ordinarily Liz would have let the remark pass, but she knew that if she let Pennell go up against Mulligan he'd get killed. She thought she had a better chance.

"All right," Early said, "let's get this solved, then."

"How?" Pennell asked. "By us drawing on one another? Winner faces Mulligan, loser dies?"

"Not quite," Mike Early said, and they all stared at him because he obviously had something in mind.

"Two bottles," Mike Early said.

They were in the saloon now, and Early had set two empty whiskey bottles on a table against a wall, so that the bullets would not ricochet after passing through the bottles.

"You'll both draw your guns and fire, and whoever shatters their bottle first wins."

"And the winner faces Dack Mulligan," Liz said.

"Right."

"Sounds more like the loser to me," Honey said.

"Is that all right with you, Alex?" Early asked.

"Fine."

"Liz?"

"Let's do it."

"Face the table."

They did so from across the room, in front of the bar. Some of the girls had discovered what was going on and had come down to watch.

"I'll call it," Early said. "Are you ready?"

"Yes," Alex said, and Liz nodded.

"On three," Early said, "One . . . two . . . three!"

Before Alex could get his gun out of his holster, Liz had shattered her bottle with one shot.

They all stared at the shards of glass on the table and the floor, some still vibrating from the impact, and then at Liz, who was holstering her gun. There was small satisfaction in shooting at bottles, but in this case if it served to keep Alex Pennell alive, then she was satisfied.

Alex gaped at her and said, "That's incredible."

"I guess I win."

Across the street in Ed Logan's office, Logan had assembled his "army," or what was left after four of his men had been killed and two others rendered useless to him because they'd had to leave town after their attack on the female bartender.

He had Tanner and twelve men . . . and Dack Mulligan.

"I'm tired of playing this easy," Logan said.

"Are we gonna just take the place, then?" Mark Tanner asked.

"They're harboring a fugitive."

"I don't know of any posters on Angel Eyes, Boss," Tanner said.

"There don't have to be posters," Logan said. "She's notorious, she's got a reputation, and we don't need her kind in Loganville. And we don't need anyone who would harbor her, or hire her."

"What about Early?"

"Mike Early's a traitor," Logan said, "and so is Alex Pennell."

"Are we just gonna kill them?" Tanner asked, worried. "What about the sheriff?"

"The sheriff is mine."

"But is he gonna stand by and watch?"

"He'll do whatever I tell him to do."

Tanner wasn't too sure about this.

"Look, Tanner, there's nobody in this town that can tell me not to do something that I want to do. I want that Angel Eyes, and anyone who gets in my way will get just what she gets. Right, Mulligan?"

Mulligan looked at Logan and said, "As long as I get paid by the head."

"You will."

One of the other men spoke up now and said, "What about the rest of us?"

Tanner started to tell the man to shut up, but Logan waved him off.

"If I come out with Angel Eyes dead and the saloon mine, every man here gets a bonus. Is that fair enough?"

There was a murmur of assent among the men and Logan assumed a self-satisfied look.

Mark Tanner was not satisfied, however. He thought that Logan was going about this the wrong way. He agreed that they should let Mulligan take care of Angel Eyes, but after that he felt that Mulligan should leave town and, without Liz Archer around to contend with, Honey's Place would soon fall into Logan's hands. He didn't think that the saloon should be forcibly taken, but he did not want to question his boss's decision. After all, he *was* paying the bills.

"All right, then," Logan said. "Mulligan, you'll start it off. The men will be on the street so that they can back you up against Early, Pennell and anyone else they may have on their side."

"I don't need any back up."

"But we need our bonus," a man said and the others agreed.

Mulligan was not a stupid man, and he did not want twelve men angry at him for taking money out of their hands. What did he care, anyway, as long as he got his money.

"All right," Mulligan said. "Let's go, then. There's no point in wasting time."

Tanner, Mulligan and the other twelve men all left Logan's office and Logan moved to his window to watch. He was the coordinator of this action, and his responsibility now was to watch and make sure it went off without a hitch.

When it did, he'd be the man who in effect had killed the infamous Angel Eyes. He felt sure he could parlay that into some sort of political career. Once he had his foot in the door he was sure that he would be on his way up.

As soon as all of this was over.

Today.

CHAPTER TWENTY-NINE

"Here comes Mulligan," Willie said, backing away from the window a bit, "and behind him is Tanner and Logan's other men."

"What are they doing?" Early asked.

"Just fanning out."

"They're going to let him make the first move," Mike Early said.

As if the townspeople knew that something was in the air, Honey's Place was curiously empty at mid-afternoon. All of the girls were downstairs, sitting at tables, watching and waiting.

"What's gonna happen now?" Lori asked from behind the bar.

"I'm going to go out there and face Mulligan," Angel Eyes said. "If I can take him, the others might back down, and without them Logan has no strength."

"So he'll hire more men and be back tomorrow," Katrina said.

"He won't hire more men by tomorrow, and by the time he does we'll have some real law in here," Liz said. "Logan will be finished if he tries to take this place by force."

"Or we will," Katrina said.

Everyone ignored Katrina's remark.

"Any of you girls want to leave, now is the time," Honey said.

"Where would we go?" Belle asked, and the others nodded.

Rita, the chunky redhead, went up to Willie and whispered into his ear, "If we get out of this alive, I'm gonna take you upstairs and fuck your brains out."

Willie's ears grew red and he stammered, "Oh, we'll get out of it, all right."

Rita smiled at him and then pressed her solid breasts against his arm and kissed him quickly on the mouth. He really was kind of cute.

Lori walked over to the boy and handed him the shotgun from behind the bar.

"Thanks," he said, and she went back to the security of her bar.

"When Logan's finished we're in business," Mike Early said.

"When Logan's finished," Liz said, staring him straight in the eyes, "so are you, Mike."

"What the hell —"

"Angel Eyes!" a voice called from the street, cutting him off. "Elizabeth Archer, I know you're in there!"

"Nobody's saying I'm not!" Liz shouted back.

"Come on out."

"Come on," Alex said, moving alongside her, "we'll go with you."

Liz didn't bother waiting to see who "we" was. She walked through the batwing doors to the board-walk outside. Behind her Pennell came out and step-ped to the left, Early to the right, and even Willie, carrying the shotgun Lori kept behind the bar.

"Well," Mulligan said, "you're even prettier than they say you are."

"I hadn't heard you were so charming," she said. "Is that going to make a difference?"

"I'm afraid not," he said, and he didn't look par-ticularly sad about it.

"I didn't think so." Liz reached into her collar for her orange bandana and pulled it out. "I don't sup-pose I could convince you to let Logan fight his own battles."

"Sorry, but I've got a living to make."

"By killing people."

"I hear you've killed your fair share."

Behind Mulligan Logan's men were spreading themselves out. Liz knew that the moment Mulligan gunned her down, they'd be firing lead into the saloon. Pennell, Early and the others wouldn't have a chance.

"I've never taken money for it."

"That's your mistake."

"Let's stop talking and get it done, Mulligan. I'm getting hungry."

Mulligan frowned because she'd said it loud enough for everyone to hear.

"Well, I hope they're serving dinner in heaven, Angel," he said, and went for his gun.

Her hand streaked for her own weapon and as she pulled it out and pointed it she saw that Mulligan had his own gun halfway. He was fast, faster than anyone else she'd ever faced — but he wasn't fast enough.

She fired as Mulligan was bringing up his gun and when the bullet struck him in the chest he froze with shock.

"Wha —" he said. He tried to lift his gun higher but it wouldn't budge, and it was getting heavier by the second. Finally, he let it drop to the ground and then fell on it, dead before he struck.

"Jesus," somebody said.

Everyone had frozen in shock.

Tanner just stared, as did the other men around him.

Up in his office Ed Logan shouted, "No!" in disbelief and pressed his face up against the glass.

Alex Pennell grinned.

Mike Early's eyes swept the street and when he didn't see Logan he looked up and spotted him pressed against the window of his office.

Liz, holding her gun ready, heard the shot and the breaking of glass. The shot came from behind her, and the glass from in front and above. She looked up and saw Ed Logan stagger as glass shattered around him, and then the man fell through the window and struck the ground with a dull thud.

She turned quickly and saw Mike Early holding his gun out.

"Put the gun away, Mike," she said, holstering her own.

He stared at her. Everyone else was still frozen, more so now that Logan was on the ground, obviously dead. Tanner and his men knew immediately that the golden goose was dead and there wasn't going to be any bonus today.

Mike Early wasn't quite ready to put his gun away, though.

"Well, Logan's finished, Liz," he said. "Tell me what you meant inside about me being finished, too."

"I'm going to tell Honey that you were playing her against Logan, and you would have gone whichever way the most money was."

"She won't believe you."

"Yes I will, Mike," Honey said, coming out of the saloon behind him. "I guess I must have known it all along, but didn't want to admit it to myself. You were the first man who ever made me think I could be in love, but that was foolish. Put the gun down, Mike."

"Not yet, not until you sign half of this place over to me. That was our deal."

"We may have had a deal, Mike, but it wasn't for half," she said.

"All right, a quarter."

"No," she said, the businesswoman in her coming out now. "You said you wanted a portion. I'll give you one percent."

"One percent?"

"And you'll leave town. Send me an address and I'll mail you your profits."

"His address is going to be prison," Liz said, "because he just murdered Ed Logan."

"He had a gun."

Alex Pennell walked over to where Logan lay and searched his body.

"No gun here."

"He must have dropped it in his office."

"There's probably one in his office, all right," Liz said, "in a desk drawer. I hardly think he had time to put it away before falling through his window."

"Better put the gun down, Mike," Alex Pennell said.

"Just remember I've got my gun already *out*."

"I still think Liz can take you, Mike," Pennell said, "and if she doesn't, I will. You can't get both of us."

From behind Early, Willie thumbed back both hammers on Lori's shotgun and said, "All three of us."

Nervously Mike Early considered his options, and in all of them he came up dead.

"Honey . . ."

"I'm sorry, Mike," she said. "I'll save your profits until you get out of jail, but don't come and pick them up in person."

She turned and walked inside.

Behind her Liz could hear Logan's army dispersing, muttering among themselves about lost money. Tanner stared at Logan's body, then reared back and kicked it.

"Dumb bastard!" he spat, and then turned and walked away with the rest of them. One more night in Sadie's House, and then he was going to leave this town behind fast.

"Mike," Liz said.

"I guess I got a little crazy," Early said, holstering

his gun. "I saw a way to finally make some money, Liz, and it didn't pan out."

"I'm sorry, Mike, but the easy way never does. You've got to make a committment one way or the other, and not play both sides."

"Liz, how about letting me ride out?"

"I'm sorry."

"Why not?"

"Because you're not better than him," she said, pointing down at Dack Mulligan. "You killed Ed Logan for money, and for no other reason."

The sheriff showed up then and stared at Logan's body in shock.

"Sheriff," Liz called.

The man looked up and frowned.

"You still are the sheriff, aren't you?"

The man shook himself and said, "That's right, ma'am, I am."

"Well, this man killed Logan in front of witnesses. He's all yours."

"Put your hands up," the sheriff said, approaching Early.

"Don't forget to take his gun," Liz said, and then Pennell was beside her and they walked into the saloon with Willie.

CHAPTER THIRTY

"Don't hold it against Lori, Honey," Liz said.

It was the following day and Liz had just finished telling Honey everything she knew, or had guessed. The saloon wasn't open yet and they were seated at Honey's table. Blossom was saddled and waiting for Liz out front, and her saddlebags were on the table.

"Those twins are really mixed up," Honey said, shaking her head. "Lori was the truly decent one and she wanted to be like Lisa. She thought Mark Tanner could teach her about sex, and she kept giving him information to get him to do it."

"He's a sick man if he needed a reason to make love to a beautiful girl like that," Liz said. "Are they going to stay?"

"They're packing up now. I don't know where

they'll go, Liz. I told them they're welcome to stay, but they say they're too ashamed."

"It's up to them," Liz said. "What about the other girls? Are they staying?"

"Yeah. In fact, I hired a new girl today."

"Oh? Who?"

"Friend of yours. Angela Pettibone."

"She left Sadie's?"

Honey nodded.

"She said she's tired of working on her back. She won't have to do that here unless she wants to."

"Well, I'm glad for her, anyway."

"What about you, Liz? Where do you go from here?"

Liz picked up her saddlebags from the table and said, "Just away from Loganville, Honey."

"It's not called Loganville, anymore."

"What's it called, now?"

"They haven't decided that, yet, but anything else will be better."

Alex Pennell came down the stairs from the second floor and walked over to where they were talking. It wasn't the first time they had seen each other that morning because they had spent the night in the same bed.

"Getting ready to leave?"

"Just about." Liz turned to Honey and asked, "Are you going to give Alex a job, Honey?"

"If he wants one, he's got one."

Honey and Alex exchanged glances and he said, "I'll have to think about it a little."

"Don't think too long," Liz said, kissing him on the cheek. "You could do worse."

Liz looked at Honey again and said, "Where's Willie? I didn't have a chance to thank him for thumbing back those hammers when he did."

"Well, as I understand it," Honey said, "Rita made him a promise yesterday, and she's been keeping it ever since."

"Well," Liz said, slinging her saddlebags over her shoulder "if he ever recovers, tell him I said goodbye."